In Love & Trouble

Alice Walker

In Love & Trouble
Stories of Black Women

A HARVEST BOOK
HARCOURT, INC.
Orlando   Austin   New York   San Diego   Toronto   London

Requests for permission to make copies of any part
of this work should be mailed to the following address:
Permissions Department, Harcourt Inc.,
6277 Sea Harbor Drive, Orlando, Florida 32887-6777.

www.HarcourtBooks.com

Some of the stories in this volume previously appeared in
*The Best Short Stories by Negro Writers, Black World,
Brother, The Denver Quarterly, Freedomways,
Harper's Magazine, Ms., Red Clay Reader.*

ISBN 0-15-602863-8

The Library of Congress has cataloged
the paperback edition as follows:
Walker, Alice, 1944–
In love & trouble.
(Harvest: pbk.)
1. Women, Negro—Fiction.   I. Title.
[PZ4.W176In3] [PS3573.A425]   813'.5'4   73-15987
ISBN 0-15-644450-X

Printed in the United States of America

C E G I K J H F D

for Muriel Rukeyser and Jane Cooper,
who listened to what was never said,

and in loving memory of Zora Hurston,
Nella Larsen, and Jean Toomer:
the three mysteries,

and for Eileen, wherever you are

Contents

Wonuma soothed her daughter, but not without some trouble. Ahurole had unconsciously been looking for a chance to cry. For the past year or so her frequent unprovoked sobbing had disturbed her mother. When asked why she cried, she either sobbed the more or tried to quarrel with everybody at once. She was otherwise very intelligent and dutiful. Between her weeping sessions she was cheerful, even boisterous, and her practical jokes were a bane on the lives of her friends. . . . But though intelligent, Ahurole could sometimes take alarmingly irrational lines of argument and refuse to listen to any contrary views, at least for a time. From all this her parents easily guessed that she was being unduly influenced by agwu, her personal spirit. Anyika did his best but of course the influence of agwu could not be nullified overnight. In fact it would never be completely eliminated. Everyone was mildly influenced now and then by his personal spirit. A few like Ahurole were particularly unlucky in having very troublesome spirits.

Ahurole was engaged to Ekwueme when she was eight days old.

—Elechi Amadi, *The Concubine*

. . . *People have (with the help of conventions) oriented all their solutions toward the easy and toward the easiest side of the easy; but it is clear that we must hold to what is difficult; everything in Nature grows and defends itself in its own way and is characteristically and spontaneously itself, seeks at all costs to be so and against all opposition.*

—Rainer Maria Rilke, *Letters to a Young Poet*

In Love & Trouble

Roselily

Dearly Beloved,

She dreams; dragging herself across the world. A small girl in her mother's white robe and veil, knee raised waist high through a bowl of quicksand soup. The man who stands beside her is against this standing on the front porch of her house, being married to the sound of cars whizzing by on highway 61.

we are gathered here

Like cotton to be weighed. Her fingers at the last minute busily removing dry leaves and twigs. Aware it is a superficial sweep. She knows he blames Mississippi for the respectful way the men turn their heads up in the yard, the women stand waiting and knowledgeable, their children held from mischief by teachings from the wrong God. He glares beyond them to the occupants of the cars, white faces glued to promises beyond a country wedding, noses thrust forward like dogs on a track. For him they usurp the wedding.

3

in the sight of God

Yes, open house. That is what country black folks like. She dreams she does not already have three children. A squeeze around the flowers in her hands chokes off three and four and five years of breath. Instantly she is ashamed and frightened in her superstition. She looks for the first time at the preacher, forces humility into her eyes, as if she believes he is, in fact, a man of God. She can imagine God, a small black boy, timidly pulling the preacher's coattail.

to join this man and this woman

She thinks of ropes, chains, handcuffs, his religion. His place of worship. Where she will be required to sit apart with covered head. In Chicago, a word she hears when thinking of smoke, from his description of what a cinder was, which they never had in Panther Burn. She sees hovering over the heads of the clean neighbors in her front yard black specks falling, clinging, from the sky. But in Chicago. Respect, a chance to build. Her children at last from underneath the detrimental wheel. A chance to be on top. What a relief, she thinks. What a vision, a view, from up so high.

in holy matrimony.

Her fourth child she gave away to the child's father who had some money. Certainly a good job. Had gone to Harvard. Was a good man but weak because good language meant so much to him he could not live with

Roselily. Could not abide TV in the living room, five beds in three rooms, no Bach except from four to six on Sunday afternoons. No chess at all. She does not forget to worry about her son among his father's people. She wonders if the New England climate will agree with him. If he will ever come down to Mississippi, as his father did, to try to right the country's wrongs. She wonders if he will be stronger than his father. His father cried off and on throughout her pregnancy. Went to skin and bones. Suffered nightmares, retching and falling out of bed. Tried to kill himself. Later told his wife he found the right baby through friends. Vouched for, the sterling qualities that would make up his character.

It is not her nature to blame. Still, she is not entirely thankful. She supposes New England, the North, to be quite different from what she knows. It seems right somehow to her that people who move there to live return home completely changed. She thinks of the air, the smoke, the cinders. Imagines cinders big as hailstones; heavy, weighing on the people. Wonders how this pressure finds its way into the veins, roping the springs of laughter.

If there's anybody here that knows a reason why

But of course they know no reason why beyond what they daily have come to know. She thinks of the man who will be her husband, feels shut away from him because of the stiff severity of his plain black suit. His religion. A lifetime of black and white. Of veils. Covered head. It is as if her children are already gone from her. Not dead, but exalted on a pedestal, a stalk that has no roots. She wonders how to make new roots. It is beyond her. She wonders what one does with memories in a brand-new life. This had seemed easy, until she thought of it. "The reasons why . . . the people who" . . . she thinks, and does not wonder where the thought is from.

these two should not be joined

She thinks of her mother, who is dead. Dead, but still her mother. Joined. This is confusing. Of her father. A gray old man who sold wild mink, rabbit, fox skins to Sears, Roebuck. He stands in the yard, like a man waiting for a train. Her young sisters stand behind her in smooth green dresses, with flowers in their hands and hair. They giggle, she feels, at the absurdity of the wedding. They are ready for something new. She thinks the man beside her should marry one of them. She feels old. Yoked. An arm seems to reach out from behind her and snatch her backward. She thinks of cemeteries and the long sleep of grandparents mingling in the dirt. She believes that she believes in ghosts. In the soil giving back what it takes.

together,

In the city. He sees her in a new way. This she knows, and is grateful. But is it new enough? She cannot always be a bride and virgin, wearing robes and veil. Even now her body itches to be free of satin and voile, organdy and lily of the valley. Memories crash against her. Memories of being bare to the sun. She wonders what it will be like. Not to have to go to a job. Not to work in a sewing plant. Not to worry about learning to sew straight seams in workingmen's overalls, jeans, and dress pants. Her place will be in the home, he has said, repeatedly, promising her rest she had prayed for. But now she wonders. When she is rested, what will she do? They will make babies—she thinks practically about her fine brown body, his strong black one. They will be inevitable. Her hands will be full. Full of what? Babies. She is not comforted.

let him speak

She wishes she had asked him to explain more of what he meant. But she was impatient. Impatient to be done with sewing. With doing everything for three children, alone. Impatient to leave the girls she had known since childhood, their children growing up, their husbands hanging around her, already old, seedy. Nothing about them that she wanted, or needed. The fathers of her children driving by, waving, not waving; reminders of times she would just as soon forget. Impatient to see the South Side, where they would live and build and be respectable and respected and free. Her husband would free her. A romantic hush. Proposal. Promises. A new life! Respectable, reclaimed, renewed. Free! In robe and veil.

or forever hold

She does not even know if she loves him. She loves his sobriety. His refusal to sing just because he knows the tune. She loves his pride. His blackness and his gray car. She loves his understanding of her *condition*. She

7

thinks she loves the effort he will make to redo her into what he truly wants. His love of her makes her completely conscious of how unloved she was before. This is something; though it makes her unbearably sad. Melancholy. She blinks her eyes. Remembers she is finally being married, like other girls. Like other girls, women? Something strains upward behind her eyes. She thinks of the something as a rat trapped, cornered, scurrying to and fro in her head, peering through the windows of her eyes. She wants to live for once. But doesn't know quite what that means. Wonders if she has ever done it. If she ever will. The preacher is odious to her. She wants to strike him out of the way, out of her light, with the back of her hand. It seems to her he has always been standing in front of her, barring her way.

his peace.

The rest she does not hear. She feels a kiss, passionate, rousing, within the general pandemonium. Cars drive up blowing their horns. Firecrackers go off. Dogs come from under the house and begin to yelp and bark. Her husband's hand is like the clasp of an iron gate. People congratulate. Her children press against her. They look with awe and distaste mixed with hope at their new father. He stands curiously apart, in spite of the people crowding about to grasp his free hand. He smiles at them all but his eyes are as if turned inward. He knows they cannot understand that he is not a Christian. He will not explain himself. He feels different, he looks it. The old women thought he was like one of their sons except that he had somehow got away from them. Still a son, not a son. Changed. She thinks how it will be later in the night in the silvery gray car. How they will spin through the darkness of Mississippi and in the morning be in Chicago, Illinois. She thinks of Lincoln, the president. That is all she knows about the place. She feels ignorant, *wrong*, backward. She presses her worried fingers into his palm. He is standing in front of her. In the crush of well-wishing people, he does not look back.

"Really, *Doesn't* Crime Pay?"

(Myrna)

SEPTEMBER, 1961

page 118

I sit here by the window in a house with a thirty-year mortgage, writing in this notebook, looking down at my Helena Rubenstein hands . . . and why not? Since I am not a serious writer my nails need not be bitten off, my cuticles need not have jagged edges. I can indulge myself—my hands—in Herbessence nailsoak, polish, lotions, and creams. The result is a truly beautiful pair of hands: sweet-smelling, small, and soft. . . .

I lift them from the page where I have written the line "Really, *Doesn't* Crime Pay?" and send them seeking up my shirt front (it is a white and frilly shirt) and smoothly up the column of my throat, where gardenia scent floats beneath my hairline. If I should spread my arms and legs or whirl, just for an instant, the sweet smell of my body would be more than I could bear. But I fit into my new surroundings perfectly; like a jar of cold cream melting on a mirrored vanity shelf.

page 119

"I have a surprise for you," Ruel said, the first time he brought me here. And you know how sick he makes me now when he grins.

"What is it?" I asked, not caring in the least.

And that is how we drove up to the house. Four bedrooms and two toilets and a half.

"Isn't it a beauty?" he said, not touching me, but urging me out of the car with the phony enthusiasm of his voice.

"Yes," I said. It is "a beauty." Like new Southern houses everywhere. The bricks resemble cubes of raw meat; the roof presses down, a field hat made of iron. The windows are narrow, beady eyes; the aluminum glints. The yard is a long undressed wound, the few trees as bereft of foliage as hairpins stuck in a mud cake.

"Yes," I say, "it sure is a beauty." He beams, in his chill and reassured way. I am startled that he doesn't still wear some kind of military uniform. But no. He came home from Korea a hero, and a glutton for sweet smells.

"Here we can forget the past," he says.

page 120

We have moved in and bought new furniture. The place reeks of newness, the green walls turn me bilious. He stands behind me, his hands touching the edges of my hair. I pick up my hairbrush and brush his hands away. I have sweetened my body to such an extent that even he (especially he) may no longer touch it.

I do not want to forget the past; but I say "Yes," like a parrot. "We can forget the past here."

The past of course is Mordecai Rich, the man who, Ruel claims, caused my breakdown. The past is the night I tried to murder Ruel with one of his chain saws.

MAY, 1958

page 2

Mordecai Rich

Mordecai does not believe Ruel Johnson is my husband. "*That* old man," he says, in a mocking, cruel way.

"Ruel is not old," I say. "Looking old is just his way." Just as, I thought, looking young is your way, although you're probably not much younger than Ruel.

Maybe it is just that Mordecai is a vagabond, scribbling down impressions of the South, from no solid place, going to none . . . and Ruel has never left Hancock County, except once, when he gallantly went off to war. He claims travel broadened him, especially

his two months of European leave. He married me because although my skin is brown he thinks I look like a
Frenchwoman. Sometimes he tells me I look Oriental:
Korean or Japanese. I console myself with this
thought: My family tends to darken and darken as we
get older. One day he may wake up in bed with a complete stranger.

"He works in the store," I say. "He also raises a hundred acres of peanuts." Which is surely success.

"That many," muses Mordecai.

It is not pride that makes me tell him what my
husband does, is. It is a way I can tell him about
myself.

page 4

Today Mordecai is back. He tells a funny/sad story
about a man in town who could not move his wife. "He
huffed and puffed," laughed Mordecai, "to no avail."
Then one night as he was sneaking up to her bedroom
he heard joyous cries. Rushing in he found his wife in
the arms of another woman! The wife calmly dressed
and began to pack her bags. The husband begged and
pleaded. "Anything you want," he promised. "What *do*
you want?" he pleaded. The wife began to chuckle and,
laughing, left the house with her friend.

Now the husband gets drunk every day and wants
an ordinance passed. He cannot say what the ordinance
will be against, but that is what he buttonholes people
to say: "I want a goddam ordinance passed!" People who

know the story make jokes about him. They pity him and give him enough money to keep him drunk.

page 5

I think Mordecai Rich has about as much heart as a dirt-eating toad. Even when he makes me laugh I know that nobody ought to look on other people's confusion with that cold an eye.

"But that's what I am," he says, flipping through the pages of his scribble pad. "A cold eye. An eye looking for Beauty. An eye looking for Truth."

"Why don't you look for other things?" I want to know. "Like neither Truth nor Beauty, but places in people's lives where things have just slipped a good bit off the track."

"That's too vague," said Mordecai, frowning.

"So is Truth," I said. "Not to mention Beauty."

page 10

Ruel wants to know why "the skinny black tramp"—as he calls Mordecai—keeps hanging around. I made the mistake of telling him Mordecai is thinking of using our house as the setting for one of his Southern country stories.

"Mordecai is from the North," I said. "He never saw a wooden house with a toilet in the yard."

"Well maybe he better go back where he from," said Ruel, "and shit the way he's used to."

It's Ruel's pride that is hurt. He's ashamed of this house that seems perfectly adequate to me. One day we'll have a new house, he says, of brick, with a Japanese bath. How should I know why?

page 11

When I told Mordecai what Ruel said he smiled in that snake-eyed way he has and said, "Do *you* mind me hanging around?"

I didn't know what to say. I stammered something. Not because of his question but because he put his hand point-blank on my left nipple. He settled his other hand deep in my hair.

"I am married more thoroughly than a young boy like you could guess," I told him. But I don't expect that to stop him. Especially since the day he found out I wanted to be a writer myself.

It happened this way: I was writing in the grape arbor, on the ledge by the creek that is hidden from the house by trees. He was right in front of me before I could put my notebook away. He snatched it from me and began to read. What is worse, he read aloud. I was embarrassed to death.

"*No wife of mine is going to embarrass me with a lot of foolish, vulgar stuff,*" Mordecai read. (This is Ruel's opinion of my writing.) *Every time he tells me how peculiar I am for wanting to write stories he brings up having a baby or going shopping, as if these things are the same. Just something to occupy my time.*

"*If you have time on your hands,*" he said today,

"why don't you go shopping in that new store in town."
I went. I bought six kinds of face cream, two eyebrow
pencils, five nightgowns and a longhaired wig. Two
contour sticks and a pot of gloss for my lips.
And all the while I was grieving over my last story.
Outlined—which is as far as I take stories now—but
dead in embryo. My hand stilled by cowardice, my heart
the heart of a slave.

page 14

Of course Mordecai wanted to see the story. What did
I have to lose?

"Flip over a few pages," I said. "It is the very skeleton
of a story, but one that maybe someday I will write."

"The One-Legged Woman," Mordecai began to read
aloud, then continued silently.

The characters are poor dairy farmers. One morning the
husband is too hung over to do the milking. His wife does
it and when she has finished the cows are frightened by
thunder and stampede, trampling her. She is also hooked
severely in one leg. Her husband is asleep and does not
hear her cry out. Finally she drags herself home and wakes
him up. He washes her wounds and begs her to forgive
him. He does not go for a doctor because he is afraid the
doctor will accuse him of being lazy and a drunk, unde-
serving of his good wife. He wants the doctor to respect
him. The wife, understanding, goes along with this.

However, gangrene sets in and the doctor comes. He
lectures the husband and amputates the leg of the wife.
The wife lives and tries to forgive her husband for his
weakness.

While she is ill the husband tries to show he loves her,

but cannot look at the missing leg. When she is well he finds he can no longer make love to her. The wife, sensing his revulsion, understands her sacrifice was for nothing. She drags herself to the barn and hangs herself. The husband, ashamed that anyone should know he was married to a one-legged woman, buries her himself and later tells everyone that she is visiting her mother.

While Mordecai was reading the story I looked out over the fields. If he says one good thing about what I've written, I promised myself, I will go to bed with him. (How else could I repay him? All I owned in any supply were my jars of cold cream!) As if he read my mind he sank down on the seat beside me and looked at me strangely.

"*You* think about things like this?" he asked.

He took me in his arms, right there in the grape arbor. "You sure do have a lot of heavy, sexy hair," he said, placing me gently on the ground. After that, a miracle happened. Under Mordecai's fingers my body opened like a flower and carefully bloomed. And it was strange as well as wonderful. For I don't think love had anything to do with this at all.

page 17

After that, Mordecai praised me for my intelligence, my sensitivity, the depth of the work he had seen—and naturally I showed him everything I had: old journals from high school, notebooks I kept hidden under tarpaulin in the barn, stories written on paper bags, on table napkins, even on shelf paper from over the sink. I am amazed—even more amazed than Mordecai—by the amount of stuff I have written. It is over twenty years' worth, and would fill, easily, a small shed.

"You must give these to me," Mordecai said finally, holding three notebooks he selected from the rather messy pile. "I will see if something can't be done with them. You could be another Zora Hurston—" he smiled —"another Simone de Beauvoir!"

Of course I am flattered. "Take it! Take it!" I cry. Already I see myself as he sees me. A famous authoress, miles away from Ruel, miles away from anybody. I am dressed in dungarees, my hands are a mess. I smell of sweat. I glow with happiness.

"How could such pretty brown fingers write such ugly, deep stuff?" Mordecai asks, kissing them.

page 20

For a week we deny each other nothing. If Ruel knows (how could he not know? His sheets are never fresh), he says nothing. I realize now that he never considered Mordecai a threat. Because Mordecai seems to have nothing to offer but his skinny self and his funny talk. I gloat over this knowledge. Now Ruel will find that I am not a womb without a brain that can be bought with Japanese bathtubs and shopping sprees. The moment of my deliverance is at hand!

page 24

Mordecai did not come today. I sit in the arbor writing down those words and my throat begins to close up. I am nearly strangled by my fear.

page 56

I have not noticed anything for weeks. Not Ruel, not the house. Everything whispers to me that Mordecai has forgotten me. Yesterday Ruel told me not to go into town and I said I wouldn't, for I have been hunting Mordecai up and down the streets. People look at me strangely, their glances slide off me in a peculiar way. It is as if they see something on my face that embarrasses them. Does everyone know about Mordecai and me? Does good loving show so soon? . . . But it is not soon. He has been gone already longer than I have known him.

page 61

Ruel tells me I act like my mind's asleep. It is asleep, of course. Nothing will wake it but a letter from Mordecai telling me to pack my bags and fly to New York.

page 65

If I could have read Mordecai's scribble pad I would know exactly what he thought of me. But now I realize he never once offered to show it to me, though he had a chance to read every serious thought I ever had. I'm afraid to know what he thought. I feel crippled, deformed. But if he ever wrote it down, that would make it true.

page 66

Today Ruel brought me in from the grape arbor, out of the rain. I didn't know it was raining. "Old folks like us might catch rheumatism if we don't be careful," he joked. I don't know what he means. I am thirty-two. He is forty. I never felt old before this month.

page 79

Ruel came up to bed last night and actually cried in my arms! He would give anything for a child, he says. "Do you think we could have one?" he said. "Sure," I said. "Why not?" He began to kiss me and carry on about my goodness. I began to laugh. He became very angry, but finished what he started. He really does intend to have a child.

page 80

I must really think of something better to do than kill myself.

page 81

Ruel wants me to see a doctor about speeding up conception of the child. "Will you go, honey?" he asks, like a beggar. "Sure," I say. "Why not?"

page 82

Today at the doctor's office the magazine I was reading fell open at a story about a one-legged woman. They had a picture of her, drawn by someone who painted the cows orange and green, and painted the woman white, like a white cracker, with little slit-blue eyes. Not black and heavy like she was in the story I had in mind. But it is still my story, filled out and switched about as things are. The author is said to be Mordecai Rich. They show a little picture of him on a back page. He looks severe and has grown a beard. And underneath his picture there is that same statement he made to me about going around looking for Truth.

They say his next book will be called "The Black Woman's Resistance to Creativity in the Arts."

page 86

Last night while Ruel snored on his side of the bed I washed the prints of his hands off my body. Then I plugged in one of his chain saws and tried to slice off his head. This failed because of the noise. Ruel woke up right in the nick of time.

page 95

The days pass in a haze that is not unpleasant. The doctors and nurses do not take me seriously. They fill me full of drugs and never even bother to lock the door. When I think of Ruel I think of the song the British sing: "Ruel Britannia"! I can even whistle it, or drum it with my fingers.

SEPTEMBER, 1961

page 218

People tell my husband all the time that I do not look crazy. I have been out for almost a year and he is beginning to believe them. Nights, he climbs on me with his slobber and his hope, cursing Mordecai Rich for messing up his life. I wonder if he feels our wills clashing in the dark. Sometimes I see the sparks fly inside my head. It is amazing how normal everything is.

page 223

The house still does not awaken to the pitter-patter of sweet little feet, because I religiously use the Pill. It is the only spot of humor in my entire day, when I am gulping that little yellow tablet and washing it down with soda pop or tea. Ruel spends long hours at the store and in the peanut field. He comes in sweaty, dirty, tired, and I wait for him smelling of Arpège, My Sin, Wind Song, and Jungle Gardenia. The women of the community feel sorry for him, to be married to such a fluff of nothing.

I wait, beautiful and perfect in every limb, cooking supper as if my life depended on it. Lying unresisting on his bed like a drowned body washed to shore. But he is not happy. For he knows now that I intend to do nothing but say yes until he is completely exhausted.

I go to the new shopping mall twice a day now; once in the morning and once in the afternoon, or at night. I buy hats I would not dream of wearing, or even owning. Dresses that are already on their way to Goodwill. Shoes that will go to mold and mildew in the cellar. And I keep the bottles of perfume, the skin softeners, the pots of gloss and eye shadow. I amuse myself painting my own face.

When he is quite, quite tired of me I will tell him how long I've relied on the security of the Pill. When I am quite, quite tired of the sweet, sweet smell of my body and the softness of these Helena Rubenstein hands I will leave him and this house. Leave them forever without once looking back.

Her Sweet Jerome

Ties she had bought him hung on the closet door, which now swung open as she hurled herself again and again into the closet. Glorious ties, some with birds and dancing women in grass skirts painted on by hand, some with little polka dots with bigger dots dispersed among them. Some red, lots red and green, and one purple, with a golden star, through the center of which went his gold mustang stickpin, which she had also given him. She looked in the pockets of the black leather jacket he had reluctantly worn the night before. Three of his suits, a pair of blue twill work pants, an old gray sweater with a hood and pockets lay thrown across the bed. The jacket leather was sleazy and damply clinging to her hands. She had bought it for him, as well as the three suits: one light blue with side vents, one gold with green specks, and one reddish that had a silver imitation-silk vest. The pockets of the jacket came softly outward from the lining like skinny milktoast rats. Empty. Slowly she sank down on the bed and began to knead, with blunt anxious fingers, all the pockets in all the clothes piled around her. First the blue suit, then the gold with green, then the reddish one that he said he didn't like most of all, but which he would sometimes wear if she agreed to stay home, or if she promised not to touch him anywhere at all while he was getting dressed.

She was a big awkward woman, with big bones and hard rubbery flesh. Her short arms ended in ham hands, and her neck was a squat roll of fat that protruded behind her head as a big bump. Her skin was rough and puffy, with plump molelike freckles down her cheeks. Her eyes glowered from under the mountain of her brow and were circled with expensive mauve shadow. They were nervous and quick when she was flustered and darted about at nothing in particular while she was dressing hair or talking to people.

Her troubles started noticeably when she fell in love with a studiously quiet schoolteacher, Mr. Jerome Franklin Washington III, who was ten years younger than her. She told herself that she shouldn't want him, he was so little and cute and young, but when she took into account that he was a schoolteacher, well, she just couldn't seem to get any rest until, as she put it, 'I were Mr. and Mrs. Jerome Franklin Washington the third, *and that's the truth!*"

She owned a small beauty shop at the back of her father's funeral home, and they were known as "colored folks with money." She made pretty good herself, though she didn't like standing on her feet so much, and her father let anybody know she wasn't getting any of his money while he was alive. She was proud to say she had never asked him for any. He started relenting kind of fast when he heard she planned to add a schoolteacher to the family, which consisted of funeral directors and bootleggers, but she cut him off quick and said she didn't want anybody to take care of her man but her. She had learned how to do hair from an old woman who ran a shop on the other side of town and was proud to say that she could make her own way. And much better than some. She was fond of telling schoolteachers (women schoolteachers) that she didn't miss her "eddicashion" as much as some did who had no learning and no money both together. She had a low opinion of women schoolteachers, because before and after her marriage to Jerome Franklin Washington III, they were the only females to whom he cared to talk.

The first time she saw him he was walking past the window of her shop with an armful of books and his coat thrown casually over his arm. Looking so neat and *cute*. What popped into her mind was that if he was hers the first thing she would get him was a sweet little red car to drive. And she worked and went into debt and got it for him, too—after she got him—but then she could tell he didn't like it much because it was only a Chevy. She had started right away to save up so she could make a down payment on a brand-new white Buick deluxe, with automatic drive and whitewall tires.

Jerome was dapper, every inch a gentleman, as anybody with half an eye could see. That's what she told everybody before they were married. He was beating her black and blue even then, so that every time you saw her she was sporting her "shades." She could not open her mouth without him wincing and pretending he couldn't stand it, so he would knock her out of the room to keep her from talking to him. She tried to be sexy and stylish, and was, in her fashion, with a predominant taste for pastel taffetas and orange shoes. In the summertime she paid twenty dollars for big umbrella hats with bows and flowers on them and when she wore black and white together she would liven it up with elbow-length gloves of red satin. She was genuinely undecided when she woke up in the morning whether she really outstripped the other girls in town for beauty, but could convince herself that she was equally good-looking by the time she had breakfast on the table. She was always talking with a lot of extra movement to her thick coarse mouth, with its hair tufts at the corners, and when she drank coffee she held the cup over the saucer with her little finger sticking out, while she crossed her short hairy legs at the knees.

If her husband laughed at her high heels as she teetered and minced off to church on Sunday mornings, with her hair greased and curled and her new dress bunching up at the top of her girdle, she pretended his eyes were approving. Other times, when he didn't bother to look up from his books and only muttered curses if she tried to kiss him good-bye, she did not know whether to laugh or cry. However, her public manner was serene.

"I just don't know how some womens can stand it, honey," she would say slowly, twisting her head to the side and upward in an elegant manner. "One thing my husband does not do," she would enunciate grandly, "he don't beat me!" And she would sit back and smile in her pleased oily fat way. Usually her listeners, captive women with wet hair, would simply smile and nod in sympathy and say, looking at one another or at her black eye, "You say he don't? Hummmm, well, hush your mouf." And she would continue curling or massaging or straightening their hair, fixing her face in a steamy dignified mask that encouraged snickers.

2

It was in her shop that she first heard the giggling and saw the smirks. It was at her job that gossip gave her to understand, as one woman told her, "Your cute little man is sticking his finger into somebody else's pie." And she was not and could not be surprised, as she looked into the amused and self-contented face, for she had long been aware that her own pie was going—and for the longest time had been going—strictly untouched.

From that first day of slyly whispered hints, "Your old man's puttin' something *over* on you, sweets," she started trying to find out who he was fooling around with. Her sources of gossip were malicious and mean, but she could think of nothing else to do but believe them. She searched high and she searched low. She looked in taverns and she looked in churches. She looked in the school where he worked.

She went to whorehouses and to prayer meetings, through parks and outside the city limits, all the while buying axes and pistols and knives of all descriptions. Of course she said nothing to her sweet Jerome, who watched her maneuverings from behind the covers of his vast supply of paperback books. This hobby of his she heartily encouraged, relegating reading to the importance of scanning the funnies; and besides, it was something he could do at home, if she could convince him she would be completely silent for an evening, and, of course, if he would stay. She turned the whole town upside down, looking at white girls, black women, brown beauties, ugly hags of all shades. She found nothing. And Jerome went on reading, smiling smugly as he shushed her with a carefully cleaned and lustred finger. "Don't interrupt me," he was always saying, and he would read some more while she stood glowering darkly behind him, muttering swears in her throaty voice, and then tramping flatfooted out of the house with her collection of weapons.

Some days she would get out of bed at four in the morning after not sleeping a wink all night, throw an old sweater around her shoulders, and begin the search. Her firm bulk became flabby. Her eyes were bloodshot and wild, her hair full of lint, nappy at the roots and greasy on the ends. She smelled bad from mouth and underarms and elsewhere. She could not sit still for a minute without jumping up in bitter vexation to run and search a house or street she thought she might have missed before.

"You been messin' with my Jerome?" she would ask whomever she caught in her quivering feverish grip. And before they had time to answer she would have them by the chin in a headlock with a long knife pressed against their necks below the ear. Such blood-chilling questioning of its residents terrified the town, especially since her madness was soon readily perceiv-

29

able from her appearance. She had taken to grinding her teeth and tearing at her hair as she walked along. The townspeople, none of whom knew where she lived —or anything about her save the name of her man, "Jerome"—were waiting for her to attempt another attack on a woman openly, or, better for them because it implied less danger to a resident, they hoped she would complete her crack-up within the confines of her own home, preferably while alone; in that event anyone seeing or hearing her would be obliged to call the authorities.

She knew this in her deranged but cunning way. But she did not let it interfere with her search. The police would never catch her, she thought; she was too clever. She had a few disguises and a thousand places to hide. A final crack-up in her own home was impossible, she reasoned contemptuously, for she did not think her husband's lover bold enough to show herself on his wife's own turf.

Meanwhile, she stopped operating the beauty shop, and her patrons were glad, for before she left for good she had had the unnerving habit of questioning a woman sitting underneath her hot comb—"You the one ain't you?!"—and would end up burning her no matter what she said. When her father died he proudly left his money to "the schoolteacher" to share or not with his wife, as he had "learnin' enough to see fit." Jerome had "learnin' enough" not to give his wife one cent. The legacy pleased Jerome, though he never bought anything with the money that his wife could see. As long as the money lasted Jerome spoke of it as "insurance." If she asked insurance against what, he would say fire and theft. Or burglary and cyclones. When the money was gone, and it seemed to her it vanished overnight, she asked Jerome what he had bought. He said, Something very big. She said, Like what? He said, Like a tank. She did not ask any more questions after that. By that time she didn't care about the money anyhow, as long as he hadn't spent it on some woman.

As steadily as she careened downhill, Jerome advanced in the opposite direction. He was well known around town as a "shrewd joker" and a scholar. An "intellectual," some people called him, a word that meant nothing whatever to her. Everyone described Jerome in a different way. He had friends among the educated, whose talk she found unusually trying, not that she was ever invited to listen to any of it. His closest friend was the head of the school he taught in and had migrated south from some famous university in the North. He was a small slender man with a ferociously unruly beard and large mournful eyes. He called Jerome "brother." The women in Jerome's group wore short kinky hair and large hoop earrings. They stuck together, calling themselves by what they termed their "African" names, and never went to church. Along with the men, the women sometimes held "workshops" for the young toughs of the town. She had no idea what went on in these; however, she had long since stopped believing they had anything to do with cabinetmaking or any other kind of woodwork.

Among Jerome's group of friends, or "comrades," as he sometimes called them jokingly (or not jokingly, for all she knew), were two or three whites from the community's white college and university. Jerome didn't ordinarily like white people, and she could not understand where they fit into the group. The principal's house was the meeting place, and the whites arrived looking backward over their shoulders after nightfall. She knew, because she had watched this house night after anxious night, trying to rouse enough courage to go inside. One hot night, when a drink helped stiffen her backbone, she burst into the living room in the middle of the evening. The women, whom she had grimly "suspected," sat together in debative conversation in one corner of the room. Every once in a while a phrase she could understand touched her ear. She heard "slave trade" and "violent overthrow" and "off de pig," an expression she'd never heard before. One of the women, the only one of this group to acknowledge her, laughingly asked if she had come to "join the revolution." She had stood shaking by the door, trying so hard to understand she felt she was going to faint. Jerome rose from among the group of men, who sat in a circle on the other side of the room, and, without paying any attention to her, began reciting some of the nastiest-sounding poetry she'd ever heard. She left the room in shame and confusion, and no one bothered to ask why she'd stood so long staring at them, or whether she needed anyone to show her out. She trudged home heavily, with her head down, bewildered, astonished, and perplexed.

3

And now she hunted through her husband's clothes looking for a clue. Her hands were shaking as she emptied and shook, pawed and sometimes even lifted to her nose to smell. Each time she emptied a pocket, she felt there was something, *something*, some little thing that was escaping her. Her heart pounding, she got down on her knees and looked under the bed. It was dusty and cobwebby, the way the inside of her head felt. The house was filthy, for she had neglected it totally since she began her search. Now it seemed that all the dust in the world had come to rest under her bed. She saw his shoes; she lifted them to her perspiring cheeks and kissed them. She ran her fingers inside them. Nothing.

Then, before she got up from her knees, she thought about the intense blackness underneath the headboard of the bed. She had not looked there. On her side of the bed on the floor beneath the pillow there was nothing. She hurried around to the other side. Kneeling, she struck something with her hand on the floor under his side of the bed. Quickly, down on her stomach, she raked it out. Then she raked and raked. She was panting and sweating, her ashen face slowly coloring with the belated rush of doomed comprehension. In a rush it came to her: "It ain't no woman." Just like that. It had never occurred to her there could be anything more serious. She stifled the cry that rose in her throat.

Coated with grit, with dust sticking to the pages, she held in her crude, indelicate hands, trembling now, a sizable pile of paperback books. Books that had fallen from his hands behind the bed over the months of their marriage. She dusted them carefully one by one and looked with frowning concentration at their covers. Fists and guns appeared everywhere. "Black" was the one word that appeared consistently on each cover.

Black Rage, Black Fire, Black Anger, Black Revenge, Black Vengeance, Black Hatred, Black Beauty, Black Revolution. Then the word "revolution" took over. *Revolution in the Streets, Revolution from the Rooftops, Revolution in the Hills, Revolution and Rebellion, Revolution and Black People in the United States, Revolution and Death.* She looked with wonder at the books that were her husband's preoccupation, enraged that the obvious was what she had never guessed before.

How many times had she encouraged his light reading? How many times been ignorantly amused? How many times had he laughed at her when she went out looking for "his" women? With a sob she realized she didn't even know what the word "revolution" meant, unless it meant to go round and round, the way her head was going.

With quiet care she stacked the books neatly on his pillow. With the largest of her knives she ripped and stabbed them through. When the brazen and difficult words did not disappear with the books, she hastened with kerosene to set the marriage bed afire. Thirstily, in hopeless jubilation, she watched the room begin to burn. The bits of words transformed themselves into luscious figures of smoke, lazily arching toward the ceiling. "Trash!" she cried over and over, reaching through the flames to strike out the words, now raised from the dead in glorious colors. "I kill you! I kill you!" she screamed against the roaring fire, backing enraged and trembling into a darkened corner of the room, not near the open door. But the fire and the words rumbled against her together, overwhelming her with pain and enlightenment. And she hid her big wet face in her singed then sizzling arms and screamed and screamed.

34

The Child Who
Favored Daughter

"That my daughter should
fancy herself in love
with *any* man!
How can this be?"
—Anonymous

She knows he has read the letter. He is sitting on the
front porch watching her make the long trek from the
school bus down the lane into the front yard. *Father,
judge, giver of life.* Shadowy clouds indicating rain
hang low on either side of the four o'clock sun and she
holds her hand up to her eyes and looks out across the
rows of cotton that stretch on one side of her from the
mailbox to the house in long green hedges. After an
initial shutting off of breath caused by fear, a calm
numbness sets in and as she makes her way slowly
down the lane she shuffles her feet in the loose red dust
and tries to seem unconcerned. But she wonders how
he knows about the letter. Her lover has a mother who
dotes on the girl he married. It could have been her,
preserving the race. Or the young bride herself, brittled

35

to ice to find a letter from her among keepsakes her
husband makes no move to destroy. Or—? But that no-
tion does not develop in her mind. She loves him.

Fire of earth
Lure of flower smells
The sun

Down the lane with slow deliberate steps she walks
in the direction of the house, toward the heavy silent
man on the porch. The heat from the sun is oppressively
hot but she does not feel its heat so much as its warmth,
for there is a cold spot underneath the hot skin of her
back that encloses her heart and reaches chilled arms
around the bottom cages of her ribs.

Lure of flower smells
The sun

She stops to gaze intently at a small wild patch of
black-eyed Susans and a few stray buttercups. Her fingers caress lightly the frail petals and she stands a moment wondering.

The lure of flower smells
The sun
Softly the scent of—
Softly the scent of flowers
And petals
Small, bright last wishes

2

He is sitting on the porch with his shotgun leaning against the banister within reach. If he cannot frighten her into chastity with his voice he will threaten her with the gun. He settles tensely in the chair and waits. He watches her from the time she steps from the yellow bus. He sees her shade her eyes from the hot sun and look widely over the rows of cotton running up, nearly touching him where he sits. He sees her look, knows its cast through any age and silence, knows she knows he has the letter.

Above him among the rafters in a half-dozen cool spots shielded from the afternoon sun the sound of dirt daubers. And busy wasps building onto their paper houses a dozen or more cells. Late in the summer, just as the babies are getting big enough to fly he will have to light paper torches and burn the paper houses down, singeing the wings of the young wasps before they get a chance to fly or to sting him as he sits in the cool of the evening reading his Bible.

Through eyes half closed he watches her come, her feet ankle deep in the loose red dust. Slowly, to the droning of the enterprising insects overhead, he counts each step, surveys each pause. He sees her looking closely at the bright patch of flowers. She is near enough for him to see clearly the casual slope of her arm that holds the schoolbooks against her hip. The long dark hair curls in bits about her ears and runs in corded plainness down her back. Soon he will be able to see her eyes, perfect black-eyed Susans. Flashing back fragmented bits of himself. Reflecting his mind.

Memories of years
Unknowable women—
sisters
spouses
illusions of soul

When he was a boy he had a sister called "Daughter." She was like honey, tawny, wild, and sweet. She was a generous girl and pretty, and he could not remember a time when he did not love her intensely, with his whole heart. She would give him anything she had, give anybody anything she had. She could not keep money, clothes, health. Nor did she seem to care for the love that came to her too easily. When he begged her not to go out, to stay with him, she laughed at him and went her way, sleeping here, sleeping there. Wherever she was needed, she would say, and laugh. But this could not go on forever; coming back from months with another woman's husband, her own mind seemed to have struck her down. He was struck down, too, and cried many nights on his bed; for she had chosen to give her love to the very man in whose cruel, hot, and lonely fields he, her brother, worked. Not treated as a man, scarcely as well as a poor man treats his beast.

Memories of years
Unknowable women—
sisters
spouses
illusions of soul

When she came back all of her long strong hair was gone, her teeth wobbled in her gums when she ate, and she recognized no one. All day and all night long she would sing and scream and tell them she was on fire. He was still a boy when she began playing up to him in her cunning way, exploiting again his love. And he, tears never showing on his face, would let her bat her lashless eyes at him and stroke his cheeks with her frail, clawlike hands. Tied on the bed as she was she was at the mercy of everyone in the house. They threw her betrayal at her like sharp stones, until they satisfied themselves that she could no longer feel their ostracism or her own pain. Gradually, as it became apparent she was not going to die, they took to flinging her food to her as if she were an animal and at night when she howled at the shadows thrown over her bed by the moon his father rose up and lashed her into silence with his belt.

On a day when she seemed nearly her old self she begged him to let her loose from the bed. He thought that if he set her free she would run away into the woods and never return. His love for her had turned into a dull ache of constant loathing, and he dreamed vague fearful dreams of a cruel revenge on the white lover who had shamed them all. But Daughter, climbing out of bed like a wary animal, knocked him unconscious to the floor and night found her impaled on one of the steel-spike fence posts near the house.

That she had given herself to the lord of his own bondage was what galled him! And that she was cut down so! He could not forgive her the love she gave that knew nothing of master and slave. For though her own wound was a bitter one and in the end fatal, he bore a hurt throughout his life that slowly poisoned him. In a world where innocence and guilt became further complicated by questions of color and race, he felt hesitant and weary of living as though all the world were out to trick him. His only guard against the deception he believed life had in store for him was a knowledge that evil and deception *would come* to him; and a readiness to provide them with a match.

The women in his life faced a sullen barrier of distrust and hateful mockery. He could not seem to help hating even the ones who loved him, and laughed loudest at the ones who cared for him, as if they were fools. His own wife, beaten into a cripple to prevent her from returning the imaginary overtures of the white landlord, killed herself while she was still young enough and strong enough to escape him. But she left a child, a girl, a daughter; a replica of Daughter, his dead sister. A replica in every way.

Memories of once
like a mirror reflecting—
all hope, all loss

His hands are not steady and he makes a clawing motion across the air in front of his face. She is walking, a vivid shape in blue and white, across the yard, underneath the cedar trees. She pauses at the low limb of the big magnolia and seems to contemplate the luminous gloss of the cone-shaped flowers beyond her reach. In the hand away from the gun is the open letter. He holds it tightly by a corner. The palms of his hands are sweating, his throat is dry. He swallows compulsively and rapidly bats his eyes. The slight weight of her foot sends vibrations across the gray boards of the porch. Her eyes flicker over him and rest on the open letter. Automatically his hand brings the letter upward a little although he finds he cannot yet, facing her strange familiar eyes, speak.

With passive curiosity the girl's eyes turn from the letter to the gun leaning against the banister to his face, which he feels growing blacker and tighter as if it is a mask that, when it is completely hardened, will drop off. Almost casually she sways back against the porch post, looking at him and from time to time looking over his head at the brilliant afternoon sky. Without wanting it his eyes travel heavily down the slight, roundly curved body and rest on her offerings to her lover in the letter. He is a black man but he blushes, the red underneath his skin glowing purple, and the coils of anger around his tongue begin to loosen.

"White man's slut!" he hisses at her through nearly sealed lips and clenched teeth. Her body reacts as if hit by a strong wind and lightly she sways on her slender legs and props herself more firmly against the post. At first she gazes directly into his eyes as if there is nowhere else to look. Soon she drops her head.

She leads the way to the shed behind the house. She is still holding her books loosely against her thigh and he makes his eyes hard as they cover the small light tracks made in the dust. The brown of her skin is full of copper tints and her arms are like long golden fruits that take in and throw back the hues of the sinking sun. Relentlessly he hurries her steps through the sagging door of boards, with hardness he shoves her down into the dirt. She is like a young willow without roots under his hands and as she does not resist he beats her for a long time with a harness from the stable and where the buckles hit there is a welling of blood which comes to be level with the tawny skin then spills over and falls curling into the dust of the floor.

Stumbling weakly toward the house through the shadows of the trees, he tries to look up beseechingly to the stars, but the sky is full of clouds and rain beats down around his ears and drenches him by the time he reaches the back steps. The dogs run excitedly and hungry around the damp reaches of the back porch and although he feeds them not one will stand unmoving beneath his quickscratching fingers. Dully he watches them eat and listens to the high winds in the trees. Shuddering with chill he walks through the house to the front porch and picks up the gun that is getting wet and sits with it across his lap, rocking it back and forth on his knees like a baby.

It is rainsoaked, but he can make out "I love you" written in a firm hand across the blue face of the letter. He hates the very paper of the letter and crumples it in his fist. A wet storm wind lifts it lightly and holds it balled up against the taut silver screen on the side of the porch. He is glad when the wind abandons it and leaves it sodden and limp against the slick wet boards under his feet. He rests his neck heavily on the back of his chair. Words of the letter—her letter to the white devil who has disowned her to marry one of his own kind— are running on a track in his mind. "Jealousy is being nervous about something that has never, and probably won't ever, belong to you." A wet waning moon fills the sky before he nods.

3

No amount of churchgoing changed her ways. Prayers offered nothing to quench her inner thirst. Silent and lovely, but barren of essential hope if not of the ability to love, hers was a world of double images, as if constantly seen through tears. It was Christianity as it invaded her natural wonderings that threw color into high and fast relicf, but its hard Southern rudeness fell flat outside her house, its agony of selfishness failed completely to pervade the deep subterranean country of her mind. When asked to abandon her simple way of looking at simple flowers, she could only yearn the more to touch those glowing points of bloom that lived and died away among the foliage over there, rising and falling like certain stars of which she was told, coming and being and going on again, always beyond her reach. Staring often and intently into the ivory hearts of fallen magnolia blossoms she sought the answer to the question that had never really been defined for her, although she was expected to know it, but she only learned from this that it is the fallen flower most earnestly hated, most easily bruised.

The lure of flower smells
The sun

In the morning, finding the world newly washed but the same, he rises from stiff-jointed sleep and wanders through the house looking at old photographs. In a frame of tarnish and gilt, her face forming out of the contours of a peach, the large dead eyes of beautiful

Daughter, his first love. For the first time he turns it upside down then makes his way like a still sleeping man, wonderingly, through the house. At the back door he runs his fingers over the long blade of his pocket-knife and puts it, with gentleness and resignation, into his pocket. He knows that as one whose ultimate death must conform to an aged code of madness, resignation is a kind of dying. A preparation for the final event. He makes a step in the direction of the shed. His eyes hold the panicked calm of fishes taken out of water, whose bodies but not their eyes beat a frantic maneuver over dry land.

In the shed he finds her already awake and for a long time she lies as she was, her dark eyes reflecting the sky through the open door. When she looks at him it is not with hate, but neither is it passivity he reads in her face. Gone is the silent waiting of yesterday, and except for the blood she is strong looking and the damp black hair trailing loose along the dirt floor excites him and the terror she has felt in the night is nothing to what she reads now in his widestretched eyes.

He begs her hoarsely, when it clears for him that she is his daughter, and not Daughter, his first love, if she will deny the letter. Deny the letter; the paper eaten and the ink drunk, the words never wrung from the air. Her mouth curls into Daughter's own hilarity. She says quietly no. No, with simplicity, a shrug, finality. No. Her slow tortured rising is a strong advance and scarcely bothering to look at him, she reflects him silently, pitilessly with her black-pond eyes.

"Going," she says, as if already there, and his heart buckles. He can only strike her with his fist and send her sprawling once more into the dirt. She gazes up at him over her bruises and he sees her blouse, wet and slippery from the rain, has slipped completely off her shoulders and her high young breasts are bare. He gathers their fullness in his fingers and begins a slow twisting. The barking of the dogs creates a frenzy in his ears and he is suddenly burning with unnamable desire. In his agony he draws the girl away from him as one pulling off his own arm and with quick slashes of his knife leaves two bleeding craters the size of grapefruits on her bare bronze chest and flings what he finds in his hands to the yelping dogs.

Memories of once
constant and silent
like a mirror
reflecting

Today he is slumped in the same chair facing the road. The yellow school bus sends up clouds of red dust on its way. If he stirs it may be to Daughter shuffling lightly along the red dirt road, her dark hair down her back and her eyes looking intently at buttercups and stray black-eyed Susans along the way. If he stirs it may be he will see his own child, a black-eyed Susan from the soil on which she walks. A slight, pretty flower that grows on any ground; and flowers pledge no allegiance to banners of any man. If he stirs he might see the perfection of an ancient dream, his own nightmare; the answer to the question still whispered about, undefined. If he stirs he might feel the energetic whirling of wasps about his head and think of ripe late-summer days and time when scent makes a garden of the air. If he stirs he might wipe the dust from the dirt daubers out of his jellied eyes. If he stirs he might take up the heavy empty shotgun and rock it back and forth on his knees, like a baby.

Everyday Use

for your grandmama

I will wait for her in the yard that Maggie and I made so clean and wavy yesterday afternoon. A yard like this is more comfortable than most people know. It is not just a yard. It is like an extended living room. When the hard clay is swept clean as a floor and the fine sand around the edges lined with tiny, irregular grooves, anyone can come and sit and look up into the elm tree and wait for the breezes that never come inside the house.

Maggie will be nervous until after her sister goes: she will stand hopelessly in corners, homely and ashamed of the burn scars down her arms and legs, eying her sister with a mixture of envy and awe. She thinks her sister has held life always in the palm of one hand, that "no" is a word the world never learned to say to her.

You've no doubt seen those TV shows where the child who has "made it" is confronted, as a surprise, by her own mother and father, tottering in weakly from backstage. (A pleasant surprise, of course: What would they do if parent and child came on the show only to curse out and insult each other?) On TV mother and child embrace and smile into each other's faces. Sometimes the mother and father weep, the child wraps them in her arms and leans across the table to tell how she would not have made it without their help. I have seen these programs.

Sometimes I dream a dream in which Dee and I are suddenly brought together on a TV program of this sort. Out of a dark and soft-seated limousine I am ushered into a bright room filled with many people. There I meet a smiling, gray, sporty man like Johnny Carson who shakes my hand and tells me what a fine girl I have. Then we are on the stage and Dee is embracing me with tears in her eyes. She pins on my dress a large orchid, even though she has told me once that she thinks orchids are tacky flowers.

In real life I am a large, big-boned woman with rough, man-working hands. In the winter I wear flannel nightgowns to bed and overalls during the day. I can kill and clean a hog as mercilessly as a man. My fat keeps me hot in zero weather. I can work outside all day, breaking ice to get water for washing; I can eat pork liver cooked over the open fire minutes after it comes steaming from the hog. One winter I knocked a bull calf straight in the brain between the eyes with a sledge hammer and had the meat hung up to chill before nightfall. But of course all this does not show on television. I am the way my daughter would want me to be: a hundred pounds lighter, my skin like an uncooked barley pancake. My hair glistens in the hot bright lights. Johnny Carson has much to do to keep up with my quick and witty tongue.

But that is a mistake. I know even before I wake up. Who ever knew a Johnson with a quick tongue? Who can even imagine me looking a strange white man in the eye? It seems to me I have talked to them always with one foot raised in flight, with my head turned in whichever way is farthest from them. Dee, though. She would always look anyone in the eye. Hesitation was no part of her nature.

"How do I look, Mama?" Maggie says, showing just enough of her thin body enveloped in pink skirt and red blouse for me to know she's there, almost hidden by the door.

"Come out into the yard," I say.

Have you ever seen a lame animal, perhaps a dog run over by some careless person rich enough to own a car, sidle up to someone who is ignorant enough to be kind to him? That is the way my Maggie walks. She has been like this, chin on chest, eyes on ground, feet in shuffle, ever since the fire that burned the other house to the ground.

Dee is lighter than Maggie, with nicer hair and a fuller figure. She's a woman now, though sometimes I forget. How long ago was it that the other house burned? Ten, twelve years? Sometimes I can still hear the flames and feel Maggie's arms sticking to me, her hair smoking and her dress falling off her in little black papery flakes. Her eyes seemed stretched open, blazed open by the flames reflected in them. And Dee. I see her standing off under the sweet gum tree she used to dig gum out of; a look of concentration on her face as she watched the last dingy gray board of the house fall in toward the red-hot brick chimney. Why don't you do a dance around the ashes? I'd wanted to ask her. She had hated the house that much.

I used to think she hated Maggie, too. But that was before we raised the money, the church and me, to send her to Augusta to school. She used to read to us without pity; forcing words, lies, other folks' habits, whole lives upon us two, sitting trapped and ignorant underneath her voice. She washed us in a river of make-believe, burned us with a lot of knowledge we didn't necessarily need to know. Pressed us to her with the serious way she read, to shove us away at just the moment, like dimwits, we seemed about to understand.

Dee wanted nice things. A yellow organdy dress to wear to her graduation from high school; black pumps to match a green suit she'd made from an old suit somebody gave me. She was determined to stare down any disaster in her efforts. Her eyelids would not flicker for minutes at a time. Often I fought off the temptation to shake her. At sixteen she had a style of her own: and knew what style was.

I never had an education myself. After second grade the school was closed down. Don't ask my why: in 1927 colored asked fewer questions than they do now. Sometimes Maggie reads to me. She stumbles along good-naturedly but can't see well. She knows she is not bright. Like good looks and money, quickness passed her by. She will marry John Thomas (who has mossy teeth in an earnest face) and then I'll be free to sit here and I guess just sing church songs to myself. Although I never was a good singer. Never could carry a tune. I was always better at a man's job. I used to love to milk till I was hooked in the side in '49. Cows are soothing and slow and don't bother you, unless you try to milk them the wrong way.

I have deliberately turned my back on the house. It is three rooms, just like the one that burned, except the roof is tin; they don't make shingle roofs any more. There are no real windows, just some holes cut in the sides, like the portholes in a ship, but not round and not square, with rawhide holding the shutters up on the outside. This house is in a pasture, too, like the other one. No doubt when Dee sees it she will want to tear it down. She wrote me once that no matter where we "choose" to live, she will manage to come see us. But she will never bring her friends. Maggie and I thought about this and Maggie asked me, "Mama, when did Dee ever *have* any friends?"

She had a few. Furtive boys in pink shirts hanging about on washday after school. Nervous girls who never laughed. Impressed with her they worshiped the well-turned phrase, the cute shape, the scalding humor that erupted like bubbles in lye. She read to them.

When she was courting Jimmy T she didn't have much time to pay to us, but turned all her faultfinding power on him. He *flew* to marry a cheap city girl from a family of ignorant flashy people. She hardly had time to recompose herself.

When she comes I will meet—but there they are!

Maggie attempts to make a dash for the house, in her shuffling way, but I stay her with my hand. "Come back here," I say. And she stops and tries to dig a well in the sand with her toe.

It is hard to see them clearly through the strong sun. But even the first glimpse of leg out of the car tells me it is Dee. Her feet were always neat-looking, as if God himself had shaped them with a certain style. From the other side of the car comes a short, stocky man. Hair is all over his head a foot long and hanging from his chin like a kinky mule tail. I hear Maggie suck in her breath. "Uhnnnh," is what it sounds like. Like when you see the wriggling end of a snake just in front of your foot on the road. "Uhnnnh."

Dee next. A dress down to the ground, in this hot weather. A dress so loud it hurts my eyes. There are yellows and oranges enough to throw back the light of the sun. I feel my whole face warming from the heat waves it throws out. Earrings gold, too, and hanging down to her shoulders. Bracelets dangling and making noises when she moves her arm up to shake the folds of the dress out of her armpits. The dress is loose and flows, and as she walks closer, I like it. I hear Maggie go "Uhnnnh" again. It is her sister's hair. It stands straight up like the wool on a sheep. It is black as night and around the edges are two long pigtails that rope about like small lizards disappearing behind her ears.

"Wa-su-zo-Tean-o!" she says, coming on in that gliding way the dress makes her move. The short stocky fellow with the hair to his navel is all grinning and he follows up with "Asalamalakim, my mother and sister!" He moves to hug Maggie but she falls back, right up against the back of my chair. I feel her trembling there and when I look up I see the perspiration falling off her chin.

"Don't get up," says Dee. Since I am stout it takes

something
second or
white heels
car. Out she
down quickly
sitting there in
ing behind me. S
sure the house is
around the edge o
Maggie *and* the hous
back seat of the car,
the forehead.

Meanwhile Asalama............ ...n motions
with Maggie's hand. Ma.............. ....s limp as a fish,
and probably as cold, des....... .... sweat, and she keeps
trying to pull it back. It looks like Asalamalakim wants
to shake hands but wants to do it fancy. Or maybe he
don't know how people shake hands. Anyhow, he soon
gives up on Maggie.

"Well," I say. "Dee."

"No, Mama," she says. "Not 'Dee,' Wangero Lee-
wanika Kemanjo!"

"What happened to 'Dee'?" I wanted to know.

"She's dead," Wangero said. "I couldn't bear it any
longer, being named after the people who oppress me."

"You know as well as me you was named after your
aunt Dicie," I said. Dicie is my sister. She named Dee.
We called her "Big Dee" after Dee was born.

"But who was *she* named after?" asked Wangero.

"I guess after Grandma Dee," I said.

"And who was she named after?" asked Wangero.

"Her mother," I said, and saw Wangero was getting

ck as I can trace it," I said.
bly could have carried it back
through the branches.
alamalakim, "there you are."
I heard Maggie say.
I was not," I said, "before 'Dicie' cropped up
family, so why should I try to trace it that far
ack?"

He just stood there grinning, looking down on me like somebody inspecting a Model A car. Every once in a while he and Wangero sent eye signals over my head.

"How do you pronounce this name?" I asked.

"You don't have to call me by it if you don't want to," said Wangero.

"Why shouldn't I?" I asked. "If that's what you want us to call you, we'll call you."

"I know it might sound awkward at first," said Wangero.

"I'll get used to it," I said. "Ream it out again."

Well, soon we got the name out of the way. Asalamalakim had a name twice as long and three times as hard. After I tripped over it two or three times he told me to just call him Hakim-a-barber. I wanted to ask him was he a barber, but I didn't really think he was, so I didn't ask.

"You must belong to those beef-cattle peoples down the road," I said. They said "Asalamalakim" when they met you, too, but they didn't shake hands. Always too busy: feeding the cattle, fixing the fences, putting up salt-lick shelters, throwing down hay. When the white folks poisoned some of the herd the men stayed up all night with rifles in their hands. I walked a mile and a half just to see the sight.

Hakim-a-barber said, "I accept some of their doctrines, but farming and raising cattle is not my style." (They didn't tell me, and I didn't ask, whether Wangero (Dee) had really gone and married him.) We sat down to eat and right away he said he didn't eat collards and pork was unclean. Wangero, though, went on through the chitlins and corn bread, the greens and everything else. She talked a blue streak over the sweet potatoes. Everything delighted her. Even the fact that we still used the benches her daddy made for the table when we couldn't afford to buy chairs.

"Oh, Mama!" she cried. Then turned to Hakim-a-barber. "I never knew how lovely these benches are. You can feel the rump prints," she said, running her hands underneath her and along the bench. Then she gave a sigh and her hand closed over Grandma Dee's butter dish. "That's it!" she said. "I knew there was something I wanted to ask you if I could have." She jumped up from the table and went over in the corner where the churn stood, the milk in it clabber by now. She looked at the churn and looked at it.

"This churn top is what I need," she said. "Didn't Uncle Buddy whittle it out of a tree you all used to have?"

"Yes," I said.

"Uh huh," she said happily. "And I want the dasher, too."

"Uncle Buddy whittle that, too?" asked the barber.

Dee (Wangero) looked up at me.

"Aunt Dee's first husband whittled the dash," said Maggie so low you almost couldn't hear her. "His name was Henry, but they called him Stash."

"Maggie's brain is like an elephant's," Wangero said, laughing. "I can use the churn top as a centerpiece for the alcove table," she said, sliding a plate over the churn, "and I'll think of something artistic to do with the dasher."

When she finished wrapping the dasher the handle stuck out. I took it for a moment in my hands. You didn't even have to look close to see where hands pushing the dasher up and down to make butter had left a kind of sink in the wood. In fact, there were a lot of small sinks; you could see where thumbs and fingers had sunk into the wood. It was beautiful light yellow wood, from a tree that grew in the yard where Big Dee and Stash had lived.

After dinner Dee (Wangero) went to the trunk at the foot of my bed and started rifling through it. Maggie hung back in the kitchen over the dishpan. Out came Wangero with two quilts. They had been pieced by Grandma Dee and then Big Dee and me had hung them on the quilt frames on the front porch and quilted them. One was in the Lone Star pattern. The other was Walk Around the Mountain. In both of them were scraps of dresses Grandma Dee had worn fifty and more years ago. Bits and pieces of Grandpa Jarrell's Paisley shirts. And one teeny faded blue piece, about the size of a penny matchbox, that was from Great Grandpa Ezra's uniform that he wore in the Civil War.

"Mama," Wangero said sweet as a bird. "Can I have these old quilts?"

I heard something fall in the kitchen, and a minute later the kitchen door slammed.

"Why don't you take one or two of the others?" I

asked. "These old things was just done by me and Big Dee from some tops your grandma pieced before she died."

"No," said Wangero. "I don't want those. They are stitched around the borders by machine."

"That'll make them last better," I said.

"That's not the point," said Wangero. "These are all pieces of dresses Grandma used to wear. She did all this stitching by hand. Imagine!" She held the quilts securely in her arms, stroking them.

"Some of the pieces, like those lavender ones, come from old clothes her mother handed down to her," I said, moving up to touch the quilts. Dee (Wangero) moved back just enough so that I couldn't reach the quilts. They already belonged to her.

"Imagine!" she breathed again, clutching them closely to her bosom.

"The truth is," I said, "I promised to give them quilts to Maggie, for when she marries John Thomas."

She gasped like a bee had stung her.

"Maggie can't appreciate these quilts!" she said. "She'd probably be backward enough to put them to everyday use."

"I reckon she would," I said. "God knows I been saving 'em for long enough with nobody using 'em. I hope she will!" I didn't want to bring up how I had offered Dee (Wangero) a quilt when she went away to college. Then she had told me they were old-fashioned, out of style.

"But they're *priceless!*" she was saying now, furiously; for she has a temper. "Maggie would put them on the bed and in five years they'd be in rags. Less than that!"

"She can always make some more," I said. "Maggie knows how to quilt."

Dee (Wangero) looked at me with hatred. "You just will not understand. The point is these quilts, *these* quilts!"

"Well," I said, stumped. "What would *you* do with them?"

"Hang them," she said. As if that was the only thing you *could* do with quilts.

Maggie by now was standing in the door. I could almost hear the sound her feet made as they scraped over each other.

"She can have them, Mama," she said, like somebody used to never winning anything, or having anything reserved for her. "I can 'member Grandma Dee without the quilts."

I looked at her hard. She had filled her bottom lip with checkerberry snuff and it gave her face a kind of dopey, hangdog look. It was Grandma Dee and Big Dee who taught her how to quilt herself. She stood there with her scarred hands hidden in the folds of her skirt. She looked at her sister with something like fear but she wasn't mad at her. This was Maggie's portion. This was the way she knew God to work.

When I looked at her like that something hit me in the top of my head and ran down to the soles of my feet. Just like when I'm in church and the spirit of God touches me and I get happy and shout. I did something I never had done before: hugged Maggie to me, then dragged her on into the room, snatched the quilts out of Miss Wangero's hands and dumped them into Maggie's lap. Maggie just sat there on my bed with her mouth open.

"Take one or two of the others," I said to Dee.

But she turned without a word and went out to Hakim-a-barber.

"You just don't understand," she said, as Maggie and I came out to the car.

"What don't I understand?" I wanted to know.

"Your heritage," she said. And then she turned to Maggie, kissed her, and said, "You ought to try to make something of yourself, too, Maggie. It's really a new day for us. But from the way you and Mama still live you'd never know it."

She put on some sunglasses that hid everything above the tip of her nose and her chin.

Maggie smiled; maybe at the sunglasses. But a real smile, not scared. After we watched the car dust settle I asked Maggie to bring me a dip of snuff. And then the two of us sat there just enjoying, until it was time to go in the house and go to bed.

The Revenge of
Hannah Kemhuff

*In grateful memory
of Zora Neale Hurston*

Two weeks after I became Tante Rosie's apprentice
we were visited by a very old woman who was wrapped
and contained, almost smothered, in a half-dozen skirts
and shawls. Tante Rosie (pronounced Ro'*zee*) told the
woman she could see her name, Hannah Kemhuff,
written in the air. She told the woman further that she
belonged to the Order of the Eastern Star.

The woman was amazed. (And I was, too! Though I
learned later that Tante Rosie held extensive files on
almost everybody in the country, which she kept in long
cardboard boxes under her bed.) Mrs. Kemhuff quickly
asked what else Tante Rosie could tell her.

Tante Rosie had a huge tank of water on a table in
front of her, like an aquarium for fish, except there were
no fish in it. There was nothing but water and I never
was able to see anything in it. Tante Rosie, of course,
could. While the woman waited Tante Rosie peered

deep into the tank of water. Soon she said the water spoke to her and told her that although the woman looked old, she was not. Mrs. Kemhuff said that this was true, and wondered if Tante Rosie knew the reason she looked so old. Tante Rosie said she did not and asked if she would mind telling us about it. (At first Mrs. Kemhuff didn't seem to want me there, but Tante Rosie told her I was trying to learn the rootworking trade and she nodded that she understood and didn't mind. I scrooched down as small as I could at the corner of Tante Rosie's table, smiling at her so she wouldn't feel embarrassed or afraid.)

"It was during the Depression," she began, shifting in her seat and adjusting the shawls. She wore so many her back appeared to be humped!

"Of course," said Tante Rosie, "and you were young and pretty."

"How do you know that?" exclaimed Mrs. Kemhuff. "That is true. I had been married already five years and had four small children and a husband with a wandering eye. But since I married young—"

"Why, you were little more than a child," said Tante Rosie.

"Yes," said Mrs. Kemhuff. "I were not quite twenty years old. And it was hard times everywhere, all over the country and, I suspect, all over the world. Of course, no one had television in those days, so we didn't know. I don't even now know if it was invented. We had a radio before the Depression which my husband won in a poker game, but we sold it somewhere along the line to buy a meal. Anyway, we lived for as long as we could on the money I brought in as a cook in a sawmill.

I cooked cabbage and cornpone for twenty men for two dollars a week. But then the mill closed down, and my husband had already been out of work for some time. We were on the point of starvation. We was so hungry, and the children were getting so weak, that after I had crapped off the last leaves from the collard stalks I couldn't wait for new leaves to grow back. I dug up the collards, roots and all. After we ate that there was nothing else.

"As I said, there was no way of knowing whether hard times was existing around the world because we did not then have a television set. And we had sold the radio. However, as it happened, hard times hit everybody we knew in Cherokee County. And for that reason the government sent food stamps which you could get if you could prove you were starving. With a few of them stamps you could go into town to a place they had and get so much and so much fat back, so much and so much of corn meal, and so much and so much of (I think it was) red beans. As I say, we was, by then, desperate. And my husband pervailed on me for us to go. I never wanted to do it, on account of I have always been proud. My father, you know, used to be one of the biggest colored peanut growers in Cherokee County and we never had to ask nobody for nothing.

"Well, what had happened in the meantime was this: My sister, Carrie Mae—"

"A tough girl, if I remember right," said Tante Rosie.

"Yes," said Mrs. Kemhuff, "bright, full of spunk. Well, she were at that time living in the North. In Chicago. And she were working for some good white people that give her they old clothes to send back down here. And

I tell you they were good things. And I was glad to get them. So, as it was gitting to be real cold, I dressed myself and my husband and the children up in them clothes. For see, they was made up North to be worn up there where there's snow at and they were warm as toast."

"Wasn't Carrie Mae later killed by a gangster?" asked Tante Rosie.

"Yes, she were," said the woman, anxious to go on with her story. "He were her husband."

"Oh," said Tante Rosie quietly.

"Now, so I dresses us all up in our new finery and with our stomachs growling all together we goes marching off to ask for what the government said was due us as proud as ever we knew how to be. For even my husband, when he had on the right clothes, could show some pride, and me, whenever I remembered how fine my daddy's peanut crops had provided us, why there was nobody with stiffer backbone."

"I see a pale and evil shadow looming ahead of you in this journey," said Tante Rosie, looking into the water as if she'd lost a penny while we weren't looking.

"That shadow was sure pale and evil all right," said Mrs. Kemhuff. "When we got to the place there was a long line, and we saw all of our friends in this line. On one side of the big pile of food was the white line—and some rich peoples was in that line too—and on the other side there was the black line. I later heard, by the by, that the white folks in the white line got bacon and grits, as well as meal, but that is neither here nor there. What happened was this. As soon as our friends saw us all dressed up in our nice warm clothes, though used and castoff they were, they began saying how crazy we was to have worn them. And that's when I began to notice that all the people in the black line had dressed themselves in tatters. Even people what had good things at home, and I knew some of them did. What does this mean? I asked my husband. But he didn't know. He was too busy strutting about to even pay much attention. But I began to be terribly afraid. The baby had begun to cry and the other little ones, knowing I was nervous, commenced to whine and gag. I had a time with them.

"Now, at this time my husband had been looking around at other women and I was scared to death I was going to lose him. He already made fun of me and said I was arrogant and proud. I said that was the way to be and that he should try to be that way. The last thing I wanted to happen was for him to see me embarrassed and made small in front of a lot of people because I knew if that happened he would quit me.

"So I was standing there hoping that the white folks what give out the food wouldn't notice that I was dressed nice and that if they did they would see how hungry the babies was and how pitiful we all was. I could see my husband over talking to the woman he was going with on the sly. She was dressed like a flysweep! Not only was she raggedy, she was dirty! Filthy dirty, and with her filthy slip showing. She looked so awful she disgusted me. And yet there was my husband hanging over her while I stood in the line holding on to all four of our children. I guess he knew as well as I did what that woman had in the line of clothes at home. She was always much better dressed than me and much

64

better dressed than many of the white peoples. That was because, they say she was a whore and took money. Seems like people want that and will pay for it even in a depression!"

There was a pause while Mrs. Kemhuff drew a deep breath. Then she continued.

"So soon I was next to get something from the young lady at the counter. All around her I could smell them red beans and my mouth was watering for a taste of fresh-water cornpone. I was proud, but I wasn't fancy. I just wanted something for me and the children. Well, there I was, with the children hanging to my dresstails, and I drew myself up as best I could and made the oldest boy stand up straight, for I had come to ask for what was mine, not to beg. So I wasn't going to be acting like a beggar. Well, I want you to know that that little slip of a woman, all big blue eyes and yellow hair, that little *girl*, took my stamps and then took one long look at me and my children and across at my husband —all of us dressed to kill I guess she thought—and she took my stamps in her hand and looked at them like they was dirty, and then she give them to an old gambler who was next in line behind me! 'You don't need nothing to eat from the way you all dressed up, Hannah Lou,' she said to me. 'But Miss Sadler,' I said, 'my children is hungry.' 'They don't look hungry,' she said to me. 'Move along now, somebody here may really need our help!' The whole line behind me began to laugh and snigger, and that little white moppet sort of grinned behind her hands. She give the old gambler double what he would have got otherwise. And there me and my children about to keel over from want.

"When my husband and his woman saw and heard what happened they commenced to laugh, too, and he reached down and got her stuff, piles and piles of it, it seemed to me then, and helped her put it in somebody's car and they drove off together. And that was about the last I seen of him. Or her."

"Weren't they swept off a bridge together in the flood that wiped out Tunica City?" asked Tante Rosie.

"Yes," said Mrs. Kemhuff. "Somebody like you might have helped me then, too, though looks like I didn't need it."

"So—"

"So after that looks like my spirit just wilted. Me and my children got a ride home with somebody and I tottered around like a drunken woman and put them to bed. They was sweet children and not much trouble, although they was about to go out of their minds with hunger."

Now a deep sadness crept into her face, which until she reached this point had been still and impassive.

"First one then the other of them took sick and died. Though the old gambler came by the house three or four days later and divided what he had left with us. He had been on his way to gambling it all away. The Lord called him to have pity on us and since he knew us and knew my husband had deserted me he said he were right glad to help out. But it was mighty late in the day when he thought about helping out and the children were far gone. Nothing could save them except the Lord and he seemed to have other things on his mind, like the wedding that spring of the mean little moppet."

Mrs. Kemhuff now spoke through clenched teeth.

"My spirit never recovered from that insult, just like

my heart never recovered from my husband's desertion, just like my body never recovered from being almost starved to death. I started to wither in that winter and each year found me more hacked and worn down than the year before. Somewhere along them years my pride just up and left altogether and I worked for a time in a whorehouse just to make some money, just like my husband's woman. Then I took to drinking to forget what I was doing, and soon I just broke down and got old all at once, just like you see me now. And I started about five years ago to going to church. I was converted again, 'cause I felt the first time had done got worn off. But I am not restful. I dream and have nightmares still about the little moppet, and always I feel the moment when my spirit was trampled down within me while they all stood and laughed and she stood there grinning behind her hands."

"Well," said Tante Rosie. "There are ways that the spirit can be mended just as there are ways that the spirit can be broken. But one such as I am cannot do both. If I am to take away the burden of shame which is upon you I must in some way inflict it on someone else."

"I do not care to be cured," said Mrs. Kemhuff. "It is enough that I have endured my shame all these years and that my children and my husband were taken from me by one who knew nothing about us. I can survive as long as I need with the bitterness that has laid every day in my soul. But I could die easier if I knew something, after all these years, had been done to the little moppet. God cannot be let to make her happy all these years and me miserable. What kind of justice would that be? It would be monstrous!"

"Don't worry about it, my sister," said Tante Rosie with gentleness. "By the grace of the Man-God I have use of many powers. Powers given me by the Great One Herself. If you can no longer bear the eyes of the enemy that you see in your dreams the Man-God, who speaks to me from the Great Mother of Us All, will see that those eyes are eaten away. If the hands of your enemy have struck you they can be made useless." Tante Rosie held up a small piece of what was once lustrous pewter. Now it was pock-marked and blackened and deteriorating.

"Do you see this metal?" she asked.

"Yes, I see it," said Mrs. Kemhuff with interest. She took it in her hands and rubbed it.

"The part of the moppet you want destroyed will rot away in the same fashion."

Mrs. Kemhuff relinquished the piece of metal to Tante Rosie.

"You are a true sister," she said.

"Is it enough?" Tante Rosie asked.

"I would give anything to stop her grinning behind her hands," said the woman, drawing out a tattered billfold.

"Her hands or the grinning mouth?" asked Tante Rosie.

"The mouth grinned and the hands hid it," said Mrs. Kemhuff.

"Ten dollars for one area, twenty for two," said Tante Rosie.

"Make it the mouth," said Mrs. Kemhuff. "That is what I see most vividly in my dreams." She laid a ten-dollar bill in the lap of Tante Rosie.

"Let me explain what we will do," said Tante Rosie,

coming near the woman and speaking softly to her, as a doctor would speak to a patient. "First we will make a potion that has a long history of use in our profession. It is a mixture of hair and nail parings of the person in question, a bit of their water and feces, a piece of their clothing heavy with their own scents, and I think in this case we might as well add a pinch of goober dust; that is, dust from the graveyard. This woman will not outlive you by more than six months."

I had thought the two women had forgotten about me, but now Tante Rosie turned to me and said, "You will have to go out to Mrs. Kemhuff's house. She will have to be instructed in the recitation of the curse-prayer. You will show her how to dress the black candles and how to pay Death for his interception in her behalf."

Then she moved over to the shelf that held her numerous supplies: oils of Bad and Good Luck Essence, dried herbs, creams, powders, and candles. She took two large black candles and placed them in Mrs. Kemhuff's hands. She also gave her a small bag of powder and told her to burn it on her table (as an altar) while she was praying the curse-prayer. I was to show Mrs. Kemhuff how to "dress" the candles in vinegar so they would be purified for her purpose.

She told Mrs. Kemhuff that each morning and evening for nine days she was to light the candles, burn the powder, recite the curse-prayer from her knees and concentrate all her powers on getting her message through to Death and the Man-God. As far as the Supreme Mother of Us All was concerned, She could only be moved by the pleas of the Man-God. Tante Rosie herself would recite the curse-prayer at the same time that Mrs. Kemhuff did, and together she thought the two prayers, prayed with respect, could not help but move the Man-God, who, in turn, would unchain Death who would already be eager to come down on the little moppet. But her death would be slow in coming because first the Man-God had to hear all of the prayers.

"We will take those parts of herself that we collect, the feces, water, nail parings, et cetera, and plant them where they will bring for you the best results. Within a year's time the earth will be rid of the woman herself, even as almost immediately you will be rid of her grin. Do you want something else for only two dollars that will make you feel happy even today?" asked Tante Rosie.

But Mrs. Kemhuff shook her head. "I'm carefree enough already, knowing that her end will be before another year. As for happiness, it is something that deserts you once you know it can be bought and sold. I will not live to see the end result of your work, Tante Rosie, but my grave will fit nicer, having someone proud again who has righted a wrong and by so doing lies straight and proud throughout eternity."

And Mrs. Kemhuff turned and left, bearing herself grandly out of the room. It was as if she had regained her youth; her shawls were like a stately toga, her white hair seemed to sparkle.

2

To The Man God: O great One, I have been sorely tried by my enemies and have been blasphemed and lied against. My good thoughts and my honest actions have been turned to bad actions and dishonest ideas. My home has been disrespected, my children have been cursed and ill-treated. My dear ones have been backbitten and their virtue questioned. O Man God, I beg that this that I ask for my enemies shall come to pass:

That the South wind shall scorch their bodies and make them wither and shall not be tempered to them. That the North wind shall freeze their blood and numb their muscles and that it shall not be tempered to them. That the West wind shall blow away their life's breath and will not leave their hair grow, and that their fingernails shall fall off and their bones shall crumble. That the East wind shall make their minds grow dark, their sight shall fail and their seed dry up so that they shall not multiply.

I ask that their fathers and mothers from their furtherest generation will not intercede for them before the great throne, and the wombs of their women shall not bear fruit except for strangers, and that they shall become extinct. I pray that the children who may come shall be weak of mind and paralyzed of limb and that they themselves shall curse them in their turn for ever turning the breath of life into their bodies. I pray that disease and death shall be forever with them and that their worldly goods shall not prosper, and that their crops shall not multiply and that their cows, their sheep, and their hogs and all their living beasts shall die of starvation and thirst. I pray that their house shall be unroofed and that the rain, the thunder and lightning shall find the innermost recesses of their home and that the foundation shall crumble and the floods tear it asunder. I pray that the sun shall not shed its rays on them in benevolence, but instead it shall beat down on them and burn them and destroy them. I pray that the moon shall not give them peace, but instead shall deride them and decry them and cause their minds to shrivel. I pray that their friends shall betray them and cause them loss of power, of gold and of silver, and that their enemies shall smite them until they beg for mercy which shall not be given them. I pray that their tongues shall forget how to speak in sweet words, and that it shall be paralyzed and that all about them will be desolation, pestilence and death. O Man God, I ask you for all these things because they have dragged me in the dust and destroyed my good name; broken my heart and caused me to curse the day that I was born. So be it.

This curse-prayer was regularly used and taught by rootworkers, but since I did not know it by heart, as Tante Rosie did, I recited it straight from Zora Neale Hurston's book, *Mules and Men,* and Mrs. Kemhuff and I learned it on our knees together. We were soon dressing the candles in vinegar, lighting them, kneeling and praying—intoning the words rhythmically—as if we had been doing it this way for years. I was moved by the fervor with which Mrs. Kemhuff prayed. Often she would clench her fists before her closed eyes and bite the insides of her wrists as the women do in Greece.

3

According to courthouse records Sarah Marie Sadler, "the little moppet," was born in 1910. She was in her early twenties during the Depression. In 1932 she married Ben Jonathan Holley, who later inherited a small chain of grocery stores and owned a plantation and an impressive stand of timber. In the spring of 1963, Mrs. Holley was fifty-three years old. She was the mother of three children, a boy and two girls; the boy a floundering clothes salesman, the girls married and oblivious, mothers themselves.

The elder Holleys lived six miles out in the country, their house was large, and Mrs. Holley's hobbies were shopping for antiques, gossiping with colored women, discussing her husband's health and her children's babies, and making spoon bread. I was able to glean this much from the drunken ramblings of the Holleys' cook, a malevolent nanny with gout, who had raised, in her prime, at least one tan Holley, a preacher whom the Holleys had sent to Morehouse.

"I bet I could get the nanny to give us all the information and nail parings we could ever use," I said to Tante Rosie. For the grumpy woman drank muscatel like a sow and clearly hated Mrs. Holley. However, it was hard to get her tipsy enough for truly revealing talk and we were quickly running out of funds.

"That's not the way," Tante Rosie said one evening as she sat in her car and watched me lead the nanny out of the dreary but secret-evoking recesses of the Six Forks Bar. We had already spent six dollars on muscatel.

"You can't trust gossips or drunks," said Tante Rosie. "You let the woman we are working on give you everything you need, and from her own lips."

"But that is the craziest thing I have ever heard," I said. "How can I talk to her about putting a fix on her without making her mad, or maybe even scaring her to death?"

Tante Rosie merely grunted.

"Rule number one. OBSERVATION OF SUBJECT. Write that down among your crumpled notes."

"In other words—?"

"Be direct, but not blunt."

On my way to the Holley plantation I came up with the idea of pretending to be searching for a fictitious person. Then I had an even better idea. I parked Tante Rosie's Bonneville at the edge of the spacious yard, which was dotted with mimosas and camellias. Tante Rosie had insisted I wear a brilliant orange robe and as I walked it swished and blew about my legs. Mrs. Holley was on the back patio steps, engaged in conversation with a young and beautiful black girl. They stared in amazement at the length and brilliance of my attire.

"Mrs. Holley, I think it's time for me to go," said the girl.

"Don't be silly," said the matronly Mrs. Holley. "She is probably just a light-skinned African who is on her way somewhere and got lost." She nudged the black girl in the ribs and they both broke into giggles.

"How do you do?" I asked.

"Just fine, how you?" said Mrs. Holley, while the black girl looked on askance. They had been talking with their heads close together and stood up together when I spoke.

"I am looking for a Josiah Henson"—a runaway slave and the original Uncle Tom in Harriet Beecher Stowe's novel, I might have added. "Could you tell me if he lives on your place?"

"That name sounds awful familiar," said the black girl.

"Are you *the* Mrs. Holley?" I asked gratuitously, while Mrs. Holley was distracted. She was sure she had never heard the name.

"Of course," she said, and smiled, pleating the side of her dress. She was a grayish blonde with an ashen untanned face, and her hands were five blunt and pampered fingers each. "And this is my . . . ah . . . my friend, Caroline Williams."

Caroline nodded curtly.

"Somebody told me ole Josiah might be out this way. . . ."

"Well, we hadn't seen him," said Mrs. Holley. "We were just here shelling some peas, enjoying this nice sunshine."

"Are you a light African?" asked Caroline.

"No," I said. "I work with Tante Rosie, the rootworker. I'm learning the profession."

"Whatever *for?*" asked Mrs. Holley. "I would have thought a nice-looking girl like yourself could find a better way to spend her time. I been hearing about Tante Rosie since I was a little bitty child, but everybody always said that rootworking was just a whole lot of n——, I mean colored foolishness. Of course we don't believe in that kind of thing, do we, Caroline?"

"Naw."

The younger woman put a hand on the older woman's arm, possessively, as if to say "You get away from here, bending my white folks' ear with your crazy mess!" From the kitchen window a dark remorseful face worked itself into various messages of "Go away!" It was the drunken nanny.

"I wonder if you would care to prove you do not believe in rootworking?"

"Prove?" said the white woman indignantly.

"Prove?" asked the black woman with scorn.

75

"That is the word," I said.

"Why, not that I'm afraid of any of this nigger magic!" said Mrs. Holley staunchly, placing a reassuring hand on Caroline's shoulder. *I* was the nigger, not she.

"In that case won't you show us how much you don't have fear of it." With the word *us* I placed Caroline in the same nigger category with me. Let her smolder! Now Mrs. Holley stood alone, the great white innovator and scientific scourge, forced to man the Christian fort against heathen nigger paganism.

"Of course, if you like," she said immediately, drawing herself up in the best English manner. Stiff upper lip, what? and all that. She had been grinning throughout. Now she covered her teeth with her scant two lips and her face became flat and resolute. Like so many white women in sections of the country where the race was still "pure" her mouth could have been formed by the minute slash of a thin sword.

"Do you know a Mrs. Hannah Lou Kemhuff?" I asked.

"No I do not."

"She is not white, Mrs. Holley, she is black."

"Hannah Lou, Hannah Lou . . . do we know a Hannah Lou?" she asked, turning to Caroline.

"No, ma'am, we don't!" said Caroline.

"Well, she knows you. Says she met you on the bread lines during the Depression and that because she was dressed up you wouldn't give her any corn meal. Or red beans. Or something like that."

"Bread lines, Depression, dressed up, corn meal . . . ? I don't know what you're talking about!" No shaft of remembrance probed the depths of what she had done to colored people more than twenty years ago.

"It doesn't really matter, since you don't believe . . . but she says you did her wrong, and being a good Christian, she believes all wrongs are eventually righted in the Lord's good time. She came to us for help only when she began to feel the Lord's good time might be too far away. Because we do not deal in the work of unmerited destruction, Tante Rosie and I did not see how we could take the case." I said this humbly, with as much pious intonation as I could muster.

"Well, I'm glad," said Mrs. Holley, who had been running through the back years on her fingers.

"But," I said, "we told her what she could do to bring about restitution of peaceful spirit, which she claimed you robbed her of in a moment during which, as is now evident, you were not concerned. You were getting married the following spring."

"That was '32," said Mrs. Holley. "Hannah *Lou?*"

"The same."

"How black *was* she? Sometimes I can recall colored faces that way."

"That is not relevant," I said, "since you do not believe. . . ."

"Well of *course* I don't believe!" said Mrs. Holley.

"I am nothing in this feud between you," I said. "Neither is Tante Rosie. Neither of us had any idea until after Mrs. Kemhuff left that you were the woman she spoke of. We are familiar with the deep and sincere interest you take in the poor colored children at Christmastime each year. We know you have gone out of your way to hire needy people to work on your farm.

We know you have been an example of Christian charity and a beacon force of brotherly love. And right before my eyes I can see it is true you have Negro friends."

"Just what is it you want?" asked Mrs. Holley.

"What *Mrs. Kemhuff* wants are some nail parings, not many, just a few; some hair (that from a comb will do), some water and some feces—and if you don't feel like doing either number one or number two, I will wait—and a bit of clothing, something that you have worn in the last year. Something with some of your odor on it."

"What!" Mrs. Holley screeched.

"They say this combination, with the right prayers, can eat away part of a person just like the disease that ruins so much fine antique pewter."

Mrs. Holley blanched. With a motherly fluttering of hands Caroline helped her into a patio chair.

"Go get my medicine," said Mrs. Holley, and Caroline started from the spot like a gazelle.

"Git away from here! Git away!"

I spun around just in time to save my head from a whack with a gigantic dust mop. It was the drunken nanny, drunk no more, flying to the defense of her mistress.

"She just a tramp and a phony!" she reassured Mrs. Holley, who was caught up in an authentic faint.

4

Not long after I saw Mrs. Holley, Hannah Kemhuff was buried. Tante Rosie and I followed the casket to the cemetery. Tante Rosie most elegant in black. Then we made our way through briers and grass to the highway. Mrs. Kemhuff rested in a tangly grove, off to herself, though reasonably near her husband and babies. Few people came to the funeral, which made the faces of Mrs. Holley's nanny and husband stand out all the more plainly. They had come to verify the fact that this dead person was indeed *the* Hannah Lou Kemhuff whom Mr. Holley had initiated a search for, having the entire county militia at his disposal.

Several months later we read in the paper that Sarah Marie Sadler Holley had also passed away. The paper spoke of her former beauty and vivacity, as a young woman, and of her concern for those less fortunate than herself as a married woman and pillar of the community and her church. It spoke briefly of her harsh and lengthy illness. It said all who knew her were sure her soul would find peace in heaven, just as her shrunken body had endured so much pain and heartache here on earth.

Caroline had kept us up to date on the decline of Mrs. Holley. After my visit, relations between them became strained and Mrs. Holley eventually became too frightened of Caroline's darkness to allow her close to her. A week after I'd talked to them Mrs. Holley began having her meals in her bedroom upstairs. Then she started doing everything else there as well. She collected stray hairs from her head and comb with the greatest attention and consistency, not to say desperation. She ate her fingernails. But the most bizarre of all was her response to Mrs. Kemhuff's petition for a specimen of feces and water. Not trusting any longer the earthen secrecy of the water mains, she no longer flushed. Together with the nanny Mrs. Holley preferred to store those relics of what she ate (which became almost nothing and then nothing, the nanny had told Caroline) and they kept it all in barrels and plastic bags in the upstairs closets. In a few weeks it became impossible for anyone to endure the smell of the house, even Mrs. Holley's husband, who loved her but during the weeks before her death slept in a spare room of the nanny's house.

The mouth that had grinned behind the hands grinned no more. The constant anxiety lest a stray strand of hair be lost and the foul odor of the house soon brought to the hands a constant seeking motion, to the eyes a glazed and vacant stare, and to the mouth a tightly puckered frown, one which only death might smooth.

The Welcome Table

for sister Clara Ward

I'm going to sit at the Welcome table
Shout my troubles over
Walk and talk with Jesus
Tell God how you treat me
One of these days!

—Spiritual

The old woman stood with eyes uplifted in her Sun-
day-go-to-meeting clothes: high shoes polished about
the tops and toes, a long rusty dress adorned with an old
corsage, long withered, and the remnants of an elegant
silk scarf as headrag stained with grease from the many
oily pigtails underneath. Perhaps she had known suffer-
ing. There was a dazed and sleepy look in her aged
blue-brown eyes. But for those who searched hastily
for "reasons" in that old tight face, shut now like an
ancient door, there was nothing to be read. And so they
gazed nakedly upon their own fear transferred; a fear of
the black and the old, a terror of the unknown as well
as of the deeply known. Some of those who saw her
there on the church steps spoke words about her that

were hardly fit to be heard, others held their pious peace; and some felt vague stirrings of pity, small and persistent and hazy, as if she were an old collie turned out to die.

She was angular and lean and the color of poor gray Georgia earth, beaten by king cotton and the extreme weather. Her elbows were wrinkled and thick, the skin ashen but durable, like the bark of old pines. On her face centuries were folded into the circles around one eye, while around the other, etched and mapped as if for print, ages more threatened again to live. Some of them there at the church saw the age, the dotage, the missing buttons down the front of her mildewed black dress. Others saw cooks, chauffeurs, maids, mistresses, children denied or smothered in the deferential way she held her cheek to the side, toward the ground. Many of them saw jungle orgies in an evil place, while others were reminded of riotous anarchists looting and raping in the streets. Those who knew the hesitant creeping up on them of the law, saw the beginning of the end of the sanctuary of Christian worship, saw the desecration of Holy Church, and saw an invasion of privacy, which they struggled to believe they still kept.

Still she had come down the road toward the big white church alone. Just herself, an old forgetful woman, nearly blind with age. Just her and her eyes raised dully to the glittering cross that crowned the sheer silver steeple. She had walked along the road in a stagger from her house a half mile away. Perspiration, cold and clammy, stood on her brow and along the creases by her thin wasted nose. She stopped to calm herself on the wide front steps, not looking about her as they might have expected her to do, but simply standing quite still, except for a slight quivering of her throat and tremors that shook her cotton-stockinged legs.

The reverend of the church stopped her pleasantly as she stepped into the vestibule. Did he say, as they thought he did, kindly, "Auntie, you know this is not your church?" As if one could choose the wrong one. But no one remembers, for they never spoke of it afterward, and she brushed past him anyway, as if she had been brushing past him all her life, except this time she was in a hurry. Inside the church she sat on the very first bench from the back, gazing with concentration at the stained-glass window over her head. It was cold, even inside the church, and she was shivering. Everybody could see. They stared at her as they came in and sat down near the front. It was cold, very cold to them, too; outside the church it was below freezing and not much above inside. But the sight of her, sitting there somehow passionately ignoring them, brought them up short, burning.

The young usher, never having turned anyone out of his church before, but not even considering this job as *that* (after all, she had no right to be there, certainly), went up to her and whispered that she should leave. Did he call her "Grandma," as later he seemed to recall he had? But for those who actually hear such traditional pleasantries and to whom they actually mean something, "Grandma" was not one, for she did not pay him any attention, just muttered, "Go 'way," in a weak sharp *bothered* voice, waving his frozen blond hair and eyes from near her face.

It was the ladies who finally did what to them had to

be done. Daring their burly indecisive husbands to throw the old colored woman out they made their point. God, mother, country, earth, church. It involved all that, and well they knew it. Leather bagged and shoed, with good calfskin gloves to keep out the cold, they looked with contempt at the bloodless gray arthritic hands of the old woman, clenched loosely, restlessly in her lap. Could their husbands expect them to sit up in church with *that*? No, no, the husbands were quick to answer and even quicker to do their duty.

Under the old woman's arms they placed their hard fists (which afterward smelled of decay and musk— the fermenting scent of onionskins and rotting greens). Under the old woman's arms they raised their fists, flexed their muscular shoulders, and out she flew through the door, back under the cold blue sky. This done, the wives folded their healthy arms across their trim middles and felt at once justified and scornful. But none of them said so, for none of them ever spoke of the incident again. Inside the church it was warmer. They sang, they prayed. The protection and promise of God's impartial love grew more not less desirable as the sermon gathered fury and lashed itself out above their penitent heads.

The old woman stood at the top of the steps looking about in bewilderment. She had been singing in her head. They had interrupted her. Promptly she began to sing again, though this time a sad song. Suddenly, however, she looked down the long gray highway and saw something interesting and delightful coming. She started to grin, toothlessly, with short giggles of joy, jumping about and slapping her hands on her knees. And soon it became apparent why she was so happy. For coming down the highway at a firm though leisurely pace was Jesus. He was wearing an immaculate white, long dress trimmed in gold around the neck and hem, and a red, a bright red, cape. Over his left arm he carried a brilliant blue blanket. He was wearing sandals and a beard and he had long brown hair parted on the right side. His eyes, brown, had wrinkles around them as if he smiled or looked at the sun a lot. She would have known him, recognized him, anywhere. There was a sad but joyful look to his face, like a candle was glowing behind it, and he walked with sure even steps in her direction, as if he were walking on the sea. Except that he was not carrying in his arms a baby sheep, he looked exactly like the picture of him that she had hanging over her bed at home. She had taken it out of a white lady's Bible while she was working for her. She had looked at that picture for more years than she could remember, but never once had she really expected to see him. She squinted her eyes to be sure he wasn't carrying a little sheep in one arm, but he was not. Ecstatically she began to wave her arms for fear he would miss seeing her, for he walked looking straight ahead on the shoulder of the highway, and from time to time looking upward at the sky.

All he said when he got up close to her was "Follow me," and she bounded down to his side with all the bob and speed of one so old. For every one of his long determined steps she made two quick ones. They walked along in deep silence for a long time. Finally she started telling him about how many years she had cooked for them, cleaned for them, nursed them. He looked at her kindly but in silence. She told him indignantly about how they had grabbed her when she was singing in her head and not looking, and how they had tossed her out of his church. A old heifer like me, she said, straightening up next to Jesus, breathing hard. But he smiled down at her and she felt better instantly and time just seemed to fly by. When they passed her house, forlorn and sagging, weatherbeaten and patched, by the side of the road, she did not even notice it, she was so happy to be out walking along the highway with Jesus.

She broke the silence once more to tell Jesus how glad she was that he had come, how she had often looked at his picture hanging on her wall (she hoped he didn't know she had stolen it) over her bed, and how she had never expected to see him down here in person. Jesus gave her one of his beautiful smiles and they walked on. She did not know where they were going; someplace wonderful, she suspected. The ground was like clouds under their feet, and she felt she could walk forever without becoming the least bit tired. She even began to sing out loud some of the old spirituals she loved, but she didn't want to annoy Jesus, who looked so thoughtful, so she quieted down. They walked on, looking straight over the treetops into the sky, and the smiles that played over her dry wind-cracked face were like first clean ripples across a stagnant pond. On they walked without stopping.

The people in church never knew what happened to the old woman; they never mentioned her to one another or to anybody else. Most of them heard sometime later that an old colored woman fell dead along the highway. Silly as it seemed, it appeared she had walked herself to death. Many of the black families along the road said they had seen the old lady high-stepping down the highway; sometimes jabbering in a low insistent voice, sometimes singing, sometimes merely gesturing excitedly with her hands. Other times silent and smiling, looking at the sky. She had been alone, they said. Some of them wondered aloud where the old woman had been going so stoutly that it had worn her heart out. They guessed maybe she had relatives across the river, some miles away, but none of them really knew.

Strong Horse Tea

Rannie Toomer's little baby boy Snooks was dying from double pneumonia and whooping cough. She sat away from him, gazing into the low fire, her long crusty bottom lip hanging. She was not married. Was not pretty. Was not anybody much. And he was all she had.

"Lawd, why don't that doctor come on here?" she moaned, tears sliding from her sticky eyes. She had not washed since Snooks took sick five days ago and a long row of whitish snail tracks laced her ashen face.

"What you ought to try is some of the old home remedies," Sarah urged. She was an old neighboring lady who wore magic leaves round her neck sewed up in possumskin next to a dried lizard's foot. She knew how magic came about, and could do magic herself, people said.

"We going to have us a doctor," Rannie Toomer said fiercely, walking over to shoo a fat winter fly from her child's forehead. "I don't believe in none of that swamp magic. All the old home remedies I took when I was a child come just short of killing me."

Snooks, under a pile of faded quilts, made a small

gravelike mound in the bed. His head was like a ball of black putty wedged between the thin covers and the dingy yellow pillow. His little eyes were partly open, as if he were peeping out of his hard wasted skull at the chilly room, and the forceful pulse of his breathing caused a faint rustling in the sheets near his mouth like the wind pushing damp papers in a shallow ditch.

"What time you reckon that doctor'll git here?" asked Sarah, not expecting Rannie Toomer to answer her. She sat with her knees wide apart under many aprons and long dark skirts heavy with stains. From time to time she reached long cracked fingers down to sweep her damp skirts away from the live coals. It was almost spring, but the winter cold still clung to her bones and she had to almost sit in the fireplace to be warm. Her deep sharp eyes set in the rough leather of her face had aged a moist hesitant blue that gave her a quick dull stare like a hawk's. Now she gazed coolly at Rannie Toomer and rapped the hearthstones with her stick.

"White mailman, white doctor," she chanted skeptically, under her breath, as if to banish spirits.

"They gotta come see 'bout this baby," Rannie Toomer said wistfully. "Who'd go and ignore a little sick baby like my Snooks?"

"Some folks we don't know so well as we thinks we do might," the old lady replied. "What you want to give that boy of yours is one or two of the old home remedies; arrowsroot or sassyfras and cloves, or a sugar tit soaked in cat's blood."

Rannie Toomer's face went tight.

"We don't need none of your witch's remedies," she

cried, grasping her baby by his shrouded toes, trying to knead life into him as she kneaded limberness into flour dough.

"We going to git some of them shots that makes peoples well, cures 'em of all they ails, cleans 'em out and makes 'em strong all at the same time."

She spoke upward from her son's feet as if he were an altar. "Doctor'll be here soon, baby," she whispered to him, then rose to look out the grimy window. "I done sent the mailman." She rubbed her face against the glass, her flat nose more flattened as she peered out into the rain.

"Howdy, Rannie Mae," the red-faced mailman had said pleasantly as he always did when she stood by the car waiting to ask him something. Usually she wanted to ask what certain circulars meant that showed pretty pictures of things she needed. Did the circulars mean that somebody was coming around later and would give her hats and suitcases and shoes and sweaters and rubbing alcohol and a heater for the house and a fur bonnet for her baby? Or, why did he always give her the pictures if she couldn't have what was in them? Or, what did the words say . . . especially the big word written in red: "S-A-L-E!"?

He would explain shortly to her that the only way she could get the goods pictured on the circulars was to buy them in town and that town stores did their advertising by sending out pictures of their goods. She would listen with her mouth hanging open until he finished. Then she would exclaim in a dull amazed way that *she* never *had* any money and he could ask anybody. *She* couldn't ever buy any of the things in the pictures—so why did the stores keep sending them to her?

He tried to explain to her that *everybody* got the circulars, whether they had any money to buy with or not. That this was one of the laws of advertising and he could do nothing about it. He was sure she never understood what he tried to teach her about advertising, for one day she asked him for any extra circulars he had and when he asked what she wanted them for—since she couldn't afford to buy any of the items advertised—she said she needed them to paper the inside of her house to keep out the wind.

Today he thought she looked more ignorant than usual as she stuck her dripping head inside his car. He recoiled from her breath and gave little attention to what she was saying about her sick baby as he mopped up the water she dripped on the plastic door handle of the car.

"Well, never *can* keep 'em dry, I mean *warm* enough, in rainy weather like this here," he mumbled absently, stuffing a wad of circulars advertising hair driers and cold creams into her hands. He wished she would stand back from his car so he could get going. But she clung to the side gabbing away about "Snooks" and "NEWmonia" and "shots" and how she wanted a "REAL doctor."

"That right?" he injected sympathetically from time to time, and from time to time he sneezed, for she was letting in wetness and damp, and he felt he was coming down with a cold. Black people as black as Rannie Mae always made him uneasy, especially when they didn't smell good, and when you could tell they didn't right away. Rannie Mae, leaning in over him out of the rain, smelt like a wet goat. Her dark dirty eyes clinging to his face with such hungry desperation made him nervous. Why did colored folks always want you to do something for them?

Now he cleared his throat and made a motion forward as if to roll up his window. "Well, ah, *mighty* sorry to hear 'bout that little fella," he said, groping for the window crank. "We'll see what we can do!" He gave her what he hoped was a big friendly smile. God! He didn't want to hurt her feelings! She looked so pitiful hanging there in the rain. Suddenly he had an idea.

"Whyn't you try some of old Aunt Sarah's home remedies?" he suggested brightly, still smiling. He half believed with everybody else in the county that the old blue-eyed black woman possessed magic. Magic that if it didn't work on whites probably would on blacks. But Rannie Mae almost turned the car over shaking her head and body with an emphatic "NO!" She reached in a wet crusted hand to grasp his shoulder.

"We wants a doctor, a real doctor!" she screamed. She had begun to cry and drop her tears on him. "You git us a doctor from town," she bellowed, shaking the solid shoulder that bulged under his new tweed coat.

"Like I say," he drawled lamely although beginning to be furious with her, "we'll do what we can!" And he hurriedly rolled up the window and sped down the road, cringing from the thought that she had put her hands on him.

"Old home remedies! Old home remedies!" Rannie Toomer cursed the words while she licked at the hot tears that ran down her face, the only warmth about her. She turned back to the trail that led to her house, trampling the wet circulars under her feet. Under the fence she went and was in a pasture, surrounded by dozens of fat white folks' cows and an old gray horse and a mule or two. Animals lived there in the pasture all around her house, and she and Snooks lived in it.

It was less than an hour after she had talked to the mailman that she looked up expecting the doctor and saw old Sarah tramping through the grass on her walking stick. She couldn't pretend she wasn't home with the smoke climbing out the chimney, so she let her in, making her leave her bag of tricks on the front porch.

Old woman old as that ought to forgit trying to cure other people with her nigger magic . . . ought to use some of it on herself, she thought. She would not let her lay a finger on Snooks and warned her if she tried she would knock her over the head with her own cane.

"He coming all right," Rannie Toomer said firmly, looking, straining her eyes to see through the rain.

"Let me tell you, child," the old woman said almost gently, "he ain't." She was sipping something hot from a dish. When would this one know, she wondered, that she could only depend on those who would come.

"But I *told* you," Rannie Toomer said in exasperation, as if explaining something to a backward child. "I asked the mailman to bring a doctor for my Snooks!"

Cold wind was shooting all around her from the cracks in the window framing, faded circulars blew inward from the walls. The old woman's gloomy prediction made her tremble.

"He done fetched the doctor," Sarah said, rubbing her dish with her hand. "What you reckon brung me over here in this here flood? Wasn't no desire to see no rainbows, I can tell you."

Rannie Toomer paled.

"I's the doctor, child." Sarah turned to Rannie with dull wise eyes. "That there mailman didn't git no further with that message than the road in front of my house. Lucky he got good lungs—deef as I is I had myself a time trying to make out what he was yellin'."

Rannie began to cry, moaning.

Suddenly the breathing of Snooks from the bed seemed to drown out the noise of the downpour outside. Rannie Toomer could feel his pulse making the whole house tremble.

"Here," she cried, snatching up the baby and handing him to Sarah. "Make him well. O *my lawd,* make him well!"

Sarah rose from her seat by the fire and took the tiny baby, already turning a purplish blue around the eyes and mouth.

"Let's not upset this little fella unnessarylike," she said, placing the baby back on the bed. Gently she began to examine him, all the while moaning and humming some thin pagan tune that pushed against the sound of the wind and rain with its own melancholy power. She stripped him of all his clothes, poked at his fibreless baby ribs, blew against his chest. Along his tiny flat back she ran her soft old fingers. The child hung on in deep rasping sleep, and his small glazed eyes neither opened fully nor fully closed.

Rannie Toomer swayed over the bed watching the old woman touching the baby. She thought of the time she had wasted waiting for the real doctor. Her feeling of guilt was a stone.

"I'll do anything you say do, Aunt Sarah," she cried, mopping at her nose with her dress. "Anything. Just, please God, make him git better!"

Old Sarah dressed the baby again and sat down in front of the fire. She stayed deep in thought for several moments. Rannie Toomer gazed first into her silent face and then at the baby, whose breathing seemed to have eased since Sarah picked him up.

Do something quick, she urged Sarah in her mind, wanting to believe in her powers completely. Do something that'll make him rise up and call his mama!

"The child's dying," said Sarah bluntly, staking out beforehand some limitation to her skill. "But there still might be something we can do. . . ."

"What, Aunt Sarah, what?" Rannie Toomer was on her knees before the old woman's chair, wringing her hands and crying. She fastened hungry eyes on Sarah's lips.

"What can I *do*?" she urged fiercely, hearing the faint labored breathing from the bed.

"It's going to take a strong stomach," said Sarah slowly. "A *mighty* strong stomach. And most you young peoples these days don't have 'em."

"Snooks got a strong stomach," said Rannie Toomer, looking anxiously into the old serious face.

"It ain't him that's got to have the strong stomach," Sarah said, glancing down at Rannie Toomer. "*You* the one got to have a strong stomach . . . he won't know *what* it is he's drinking."

Rannie Toomer began to tremble way down deep in her stomach. It sure was weak, she thought. Trembling like that. But what could she mean her Snooks to drink? Not cat's blood—! And not some of the messes with bat's wings she'd heard Sarah mixed for people sick in the head? . . .

"What is it?" she whispered, bringing her head close to Sarah's knee. Sarah leaned down and put her toothless mouth to her ear.

"The only thing that can save this child now is some good strong horse tea," she said, keeping her eyes on the girl's face. "The *only* thing. And if you wants him out of that bed you better make tracks to git some."

Rannie Toomer took up her wet coat and stepped across the porch into the pasture. The rain fell against her face with the force of small hailstones. She started walking in the direction of the trees where she could see the bulky lightish shapes of cows. Her thin plastic shoes were sucked at by the mud, but she pushed herself forward in search of the lone gray mare.

All the animals shifted ground and rolled big dark eyes at Rannie Toomer. She made as little noise as she could and leaned against a tree to wait.

Thunder rose from the side of the sky like tires of a big truck rumbling over rough dirt road. Then it stood a split second in the middle of the sky before it exploded like a giant firecracker, then rolled away again like an empty keg. Lightning streaked across the sky, setting the air white and charged.

Rannie Toomer stood dripping under her tree, hoping not to be struck. She kept her eyes carefully on the behind of the gray mare, who, after nearly an hour, began nonchalantly to spread her muddy knees.

At that moment Rannie Toomer realized that she had brought nothing to catch the precious tea in. Lightning struck something not far off and caused a crackling and groaning in the woods that frightened the animals away from their shelter. Rannie Toomer slipped down in the mud trying to take off one of her plastic shoes to catch the tea. And the gray mare, trickling some, broke for a clump of cedars yards away.

Rannie Toomer was close enough to catch the tea if she could keep up with the mare while she ran. So alternately holding her breath and gasping for air she started after her. Mud from her fall clung to her elbows and streaked her frizzy hair. Slipping and sliding in the mud she raced after the mare, holding out, as if for alms, her plastic shoe.

In the house Sarah sat, her shawls and sweaters tight around her, rubbing her knees and muttering under her breath. She heard the thunder, saw the lightning that lit up the dingy room and turned her waiting face to the bed. Hobbling over on stiff legs she could hear no sound; the frail breathing had stopped with the thunder, not to come again.

Across the mud-washed pasture Rannie Toomer stumbled, holding out her plastic shoe for the gray mare to fill. In spurts and splashes mixed with rainwater she gathered her tea. In parting, the old mare snorted and threw up one big leg, knocking her back into the mud. She rose, trembling and crying, holding the shoe, spilling none over the top but realizing a leak, a tiny crack at her shoe's front. Quickly she stuck her mouth there,

over the crack, and ankle deep in the slippery mud of
the pasture and freezing in her shabby wet coat, she ran
home to give the still warm horse tea to her baby
Snooks.

Entertaining God

I

John, the son. Loving the God given him.

The boy huffed and puffed and swatted flies as he climbed the hill, pulling on the rope. He stumbled on the uneven ground, a pile of grit and gravel collected in the toe of his shoe. He could not stop to empty out his shoe, nor could he stop to rest, because he did not have the time. It was getting late in the afternoon and there was a chance the gorilla would be missed. He hoped he would not be missed until at least tomorrow, which would give him time. He jerked on the rope. He would have to reach the top of the high hill very soon or the gorilla was going to fall down and go to sleep right where he was.

"C'mon," he said encouragingly to the gorilla, who looked at him with dreamy yellow eyes. He had been talking to him soothingly all the way but the gorilla was drowsy from the medicine the zoo keepers had given him and did not reply except to grunt sluggishly deep in his throat. He hoped to have better luck with him when he woke up tomorrow.

All around them now were trees and grass and vines and he hoped the scenery was pleasing to the gorilla. It was pleasing to him, and he was *himself* a person; who did not need trees and grass and vines. There was a faint drone from the direction of the highway as cars whizzed to and fro around the outer edges of the zoo. They sounded, he thought, like wasps or big flies, as he swatted at the gnats that were hanging around his face, Behind him he felt a tugging on the rope as the gorilla cleared the air in front of his face, too, but with a sluggish petulant swipe, and his black plastic eyelids had started to droop.

The boy leading the gorilla was young and very lean, with exceptionally black skin that seemed to curve light around his bones. The skin of his face was stretched taut by the pointed severity of his cheeks, and this flattened his nose, which was broad and rounded at the tip.

There was a wistful gentleness in his face, an effortless grace in the erect way he held his head. It was not apparent, in his stride, what he had suffered. Those first days at the zoo, when he stood crying in front of the gorilla cage, had left no lines of agony on his face. The hour of his deliverance was not stamped forever on his forehead; when he embraced the God that others—his mother—had chosen for him.

The boy tugged hard at the rope; they were going over a big lump of ground that was a half-submerged rock. The gorilla stopped abruptly, sniffed resentfully at the boy, and without further notice sat down on the ground. The boy pulled the rope once more but the gorilla didn't budge and instead stretched himself out sullenly and fell asleep. Soon he began to snore, which caused the boy to stand over him and look wonderingly into his open mouth. It was deep rose and pink inside, trimmed in black, like a pretty cave. His big swooping teeth were like yellowed icicles and rusty stalagmites. There was a sturdy bush nearby to which the boy fastened the end of the rope, looking back momentarily at the mouth. Then he raked together leaves and grass and branches to make the place where they would spend the night more comfortable. Then he took from under his shirt half a loaf of rye bread and a small bottle half full of red wine. He laid them carefully underneath the bush around which he had tied the rope. Then he left the gorilla sleeping as he walked away from their camp-site to try to figure out where they were.

They were still within the grounds of the Bronx Zoo, that much he knew, for they had not yet come up against the high fence that surrounded the zoo. However, it was not his intention to get outside the zoo, so this did not bother him. He hoped that if the zoo keepers missed the gorilla before nightfall they would think he had been taken out of the area, for that would keep them safe until he had got what he wanted from the gorilla, and the gorilla would have received the kind of homage he deserved from him.

He satisfied himself that he would be able to spot searchers if they started up the hill toward them. There were trees and shrubs and vines and large boulders, and if necessary—and if he could arouse the gorilla—they could move about and lose anyone who came after them. But for the present he was not worried for he did not expect the gorilla to be missed until feeding time tomorrow and by then everything would be over.

The boy walked back to the gorilla and sat down on the grass. Dusk had begun to fall while he made his survey and now it was quite dark. Like a drunken old man the gorilla snorted and grumbled in his sleep. The boy supposed it was the medicine. Each year about this time the gorillas in the zoo got a dose of something to protect them from diseases and it doped them up for a couple of days. That was how he had been able to get this one out of his cage without bringing down the whole zoo; gorillas could be noisy when alert. The boy smiled down at the black hulk of fur next to him. He looked in awe at the size of this beautiful animal. Gently he rubbed the gorilla across the back of the neck and the gorilla snorted, then sighed in complete comfort and abandonment like a huge sleepy baby. The boy stretched out next to him, laughing out loud. Soon he fell asleep and as the air got cooler toward the middle of the night he snuggled closer and closer to the clean warm fur of the big ape.

He slept dreamlessly and greeted the slow windless dawn with keen anticipation. The gorilla was still asleep, but less peacefully now. The boy thought the medicine must be just about worn off. He stood on the lump of ground over the head of the gorilla and looked in the direction of the zoo buildings and of the building from which he had taken the gorilla. All was quiet, the forest all around was still. He listened intently, waiting. Soon the birds began to chirp and the wind stirred, moving the leaves. The very air seemed alive. It was like singing or flying and the boy felt exhilarated. He stretched his hands above his head as high as they would go as he greeted the sun, which rose in slow distant majesty across a misty sky, nudging clouds gently as it made its way. The boy stared straight at the sun through the mists, delighted at the sunlike spots that stayed in his head and danced before his eyes. The gorilla began to grunt and rake his blunt claws against the ground. The boy watched him with eyes shining with great pride. He turned away as the gorilla sat up and began picking at his coat, and proceeded to gather small twigs and moss with which to start a fire.

The gorilla sat upright, grumpily watching and picking at his hide, his bleary eyes clearing gradually like the sky. He sniffed the air, looked around him at the forest, looked in stupid bewilderment at the open sky which extended on and on in blueness the farther back he reared his head. He rolled his giant head round on his neck as if chasing away the remains of a headache. He pressed lightly against the place on his buttocks where the big hypo had gone in. He grunted loudly and impatiently. He was hungry.

The boy went about building the fire with slow ritualistic movements, his black hands caressing the wood, the leaves, his warm breath moving the fine feathery dryness of the moss. His wide bottom lip hung open in concentration. From time to time he looked up at the gorilla and smiled burstingly in suppressed jubilation.

Soon the small fire was blazing. The boy sat back from it and looked at the gorilla. He smiled. The gorilla grunted. He turned distrustingly away from the fire, then turned back to it as the boy went over to the bush, took the bag with the bread in it and walked back toward the fire. The gorilla began to fret and strain

IN LOVE & TROUBLE

against his rope. He smelled the bread as it came from the wrapper and made a move toward it. The rope drew him up short.

"Just you wait a minute, you," the boy said softly, and gingerly held the bread over the flame. In a second he leaped up as if he had forgotten something important. He put the bread down and untied the gorilla. He led him to the shallow rise overlooking the fire and gently pushed him down. The gorilla, as if still doped and continually wringing his head on his neck, sat tamely. The boy resumed his toasting of the bread. As each piece of bread was thoroughly blackened he dropped it into the flames. Then, as the bread burned, he bowed all the way down to the ground in front of the gorilla, who sat like a hairy mystified Buddha on the shallow ledge, his greedy eyes wide in awe of the flames. Each time the boy took out a new piece of bread from the bag and the odor of rye reached him the gorilla made a move forward, slowly and hopelessly, like a turtle. The boy kept toasting the bread, then dropping it in the fire, then bowing his head to the ground. The gorilla watched. The boy mumbled all the while. When he got to the last piece of bread he halted in his prayers and reached behind him for the wine. He opened the bottle and the scent, like roses and vinegar, wafted up in the air and reached the gorilla, who became thoroughly awake for the first time. The boy bowed his dark woolly head to the ground once more, mumble, mumble, mumble, then toasted the endpiece of bread. Then, holding the bread in his hand, burned to a crisp, he poured the half-bottle of wine into the fire. The gorilla, who had watched everything as if spellbound, gave a gruff howl of fierce disapproval.

With his back to the sodden embers the boy bowed on his knees, still mumbling his long fervent prayer. On his knees he dragged his body up to the gorilla's feet. The gorilla's feet were black and rough like his own, with long scaly toes and straight silken hair on top that was not like his. Reverently, he lay the burnt offering at the feet of his savage idol. And the gorilla's feet, powerful and large and twitching with impatience, were the last things he saw before he was hurled out of the violent jungle of the world into nothingness and a blinding light. And the gorilla, snorting with disgust, grabbed the bread.

2

The life of John's father, another place, ending.

John's father had heard that in that last miserable second your whole life passed before your eyes. But he and the plain black girl who was his second wife moved into the moment itself with few reflections to spare. When they heard the twister coming, like twenty wild trains slamming through the houses on their block, she grabbed the baby and he the small boy and hardly noticing that the other moved each ran toward the refrigerator, frantically pulling out the meager dishes of food, flinging a half-empty carton of milk across the room, and making a place where the vegetables and fruits should have been for the two children to crouch. With no tears, no warnings, no good-byes, they slammed the door.

Minutes after the cyclone had leveled the street to

the ground searchers would come and find the children still huddled inside the refrigerator. Almost dead, cold, the baby crying and gasping for air, the small boy numb with horror and with chill. They would peer out not into the familiar shabby kitchen but into an open field. Perhaps the church or the Red Cross or a kind neighbor would take them in, bed them down among other children similarly lost, and in twenty years the plain black girl and the man who was their father would be forgotten, recalled, if even briefly, by sudden forceful enclosures in damp and chilly places.

This, too, the future, passed before his eyes, and not one past life but two. He wondered, in that moment, only fleetingly of the God he'd sworn to serve and of the wife he held now in his arms, and thought instead of his first wife, the librarian, and of their son, John.

He had married his first wife in a gigantic two-ring ceremony, in a church, and his wife had had the wedding pictures touched up so that he did not resemble himself. In the pictures his skin was olive brown and smooth when in fact it was black and stubbly and rough. He had married his wife because she was light and loose and fun and because she had long red hair. After they were married she stopped dyeing it and let it grow out black. Then, with the black unimaginative hair and the discreet black patent-leather shoes she wore, the gray suits she seemed to love, the continual poking into books—well, she was just no longer anyone he recognized.

After he quit the post office he became a hairdresser. He liked being around women. Old women with three chins who wanted blue or purple hair, young tacky girls who adored the way platinum sparkled against black skin, even stolid reserved librarians like his wife who never seemed to want anything but a continuation of the way they were. Women like his wife intrigued him because the duller he could make them look the more respectable they felt, and the better they liked it. But living with his wife was more difficult than straightening her hair every two weeks. He could conquer the kinks in her hair but her body and mind became rapidly harder to penetrate. He found the struggle humiliating besides.

John, unfortunately, had been too small to hold his interest. Which was not to acknowledge lack of love, simply lack of interest.

The plain black girl he married next was a sister in the Nation and would not agree to go away with him except to some forsaken place where they could preach the Word to those of their people who had formerly floundered without it. He too changed his name and took an X. He was not comfortable with the X, however, because he began to feel each morning that the day before he had not existed. When his anxiety did not subside his wife claimed an inability to comprehend the persistent stubbornness of his agony. He knew what it was, of course; without a last name John would never be able to find him.

He had seen the boy once in ten years, when John was almost fifteen years old. He had been eager to talk to John, eager to please. John was eager to get away from him. Not from dislike or out of anger, that was clear. John did not blame his father for deserting him, at least that is what he said. No, John simply wanted to get up to the Bronx Zoo before it closed.

"John, I don't understand!" he had shouted, annoyed

to find himself in competition with a zoo. His son watched his lips move with a curious interest, as if he could not possibly hear the words coming out. John looked at his father with impatience and pity, and with an expression faintly contemptuous, superior. It unnerved him, for it was the way John himself had been looked at when he was a baby. For John had all the physical characteristics that in the Western world are scorned. John looked like his father. An honest black. His forehead sloped backward from the bridge of his eyes. His nose was flat, his mouth too wide. John's mother was always fussing over John but hated him because he looked like his father instead of like her. She blamed her husband for what he had "done to" John. Yet he was John's father, why shouldn't the boy resemble him?

His new wife loved him fiercely, with a kind of passionate abstraction, as if he were a painting or wondrous sculpture. She wore his color and the construction of his features like a badge. She saw him as a king returning to his lands and was bitterly proud of whatever their two bodies produced.

In the South, in a hate-filled state complete with magnolias, tornadoes and broken-tongued field hands, they had settled down to raise a family of their own. The minds of their people were as harsh and flat as the land and had little time to absorb a new religion more dangerous than the old. Still, they had persisted; and in the struggle he found peace for himself. It was true that he was lost to John, but through the years his wife helped him see that John was really just a cipher, one of the millions who needed the truth their religion could bring. He had finally accepted himself, but it seemed that in the moment the beauty of this acceptance was most clear he must say good-bye to it.

A sound like twenty wild trains rushed through the street. They moved as one person will move, their children in their arms, toward the refrigerator. They threw out the food, crammed the children in. They slammed the refrigerator door and rushed, like children themselves, into each other's arms.

3

The mother of John, searching . . .

Of course John's mother was much older than the other black radical poets. She was in her forties and most of them were in their twenties or early thirties. She looked young, though, and engaged in the same kind of inflammatory rhetoric they did. She became very popular on the circuit because she said pithy, pungent, unexpected things, and because she undermined the other poets in hilarious and harmless ways. Students who heard her read almost always laughed loudly and raised their fists and stomped and yelled "Right on!" This was extremely gratifying to her, because she wanted more than anything in the world a rapport with people younger than herself. This is not to suggest she used the Black revolution to bridge the generation gap, but rather that she found it the ideal vehicle from which to vindicate herself from former ways of error.

No, she had not, as several of the other poets claimed, truly believed in nonviolence or Martin Luther King (she had found his Southern accent offensive and his Christian calling ludicrous), nor had she ever worked as a token Negro in a white-owned corporation. She had never attended an interracial affair at which she was the only black, and it went without saying that all her love affairs had been correct.

On the other hand, her marriage to a lower echelon post-office functionary, who, though black indeed, was not suited for her temperamentally, foundered for many years, and shortly after the birth of a son was completely submerged. And though she was heard from coast to coast blasting the genteel Southern college she had attended for stunting her revolutionary growth and encouraging her incipient whiteness, and striking out at black preachers, teachers and leaders for being "eunuchs," "Oreos," and "fruits," it was actually the son of her unsuccessful marriage that lent fire to her poetic deliveries. He was never mentioned, of course, and none of the students to whom she lectured and read her poetry knew of his existence.

He had been dead for three or four years before she even began to think of writing poetry; before that time she had been assistant librarian at the Carver branch of the Municipal Library of New York City. Her son had died at the age of fifteen under rather peculiar circumstances—after removing a large and ferocious gorilla from its cage in the Bronx Zoo. Only his mother had been able to piece together the details of his death. She did not like to talk about it, however, and spent two months in a sanitarium afterward, tying a knot over and over in one of her nylons to make a small boy's stocking cap.

A year after she was released from the sanitarium she cut her chignoned hair, discarded her high-heel patents for sandals and boots, and bought her first pair of large hoop earrings for a dollar and fifty cents. A short time later she bought a dozen yards of African print material and made herself several bright nunnish dresses. And, in a bout of agony one day she drew small, elaborate sacrification marks down her cheeks. She also tried going without a bra, but since she was well built with good-sized breasts, going braless caused backache, and she had to give it up. She did, however, throw away her girdle for good.

She might have been a spectacularly striking figure, with her cropped fluffy hair and her tall, statuesque body—her skin was good and surprisingly the sacrification marks played up the noble severity of her cheekbones—but her eyes were too small and tended to glint, giving her a suspicious, beady-eyed look, the look of pouncing, of grabbing hold.

The students who applauded so actively during her readings almost never stopped afterward to talk with her, and even after standing ovations she left the lecture halls unescorted, for even the department heads who invited her found a reason, usually, to slip out and away minutes before she brought her delivery to a close. She received all payments for her readings in the mail.

And sometimes, after she'd watched the students turn and go outside, laughing and joking among themselves, puffing out their chests in the new proud blackness and identification with their beauty her poetry had given them, she leaned against the lectern and put her hands up to her eyes, feeling a weakness in her legs and an ache in her throat. And at these times she almost always saw her son sitting in one of the back rows in front of her, his hands folded in his lap, his eyes bright with enthusiasm for her teachings, his thin young back straight.

She had renamed him Jomo after his death. Softly she would call to him, "John?" "John?" "*Jomo?*" And though he never answered her he would amble down to the lectern and stand waiting while she gathered up her notes, her poems, her clippings from newspapers (her voluminous collection of the errors of others). He would wait for her to wipe her eyes. Then he would go with her as far as the door.

The Diary of
an African Nun

Our mission school is at the foot of lovely Uganda mountains and is a resting place for travelers. Classrooms in daylight, a hotel when the sun sets.

The question is in the eyes of all who come here: Why are you—so young, so beautiful (perhaps)—a nun? The Americans cannot understand my humility. I bring them clean sheets and towels and return their too much money and candid smiles. The Germans are very different. They do not offer money but praise. The sight of a black nun strikes their sentimentality; and, as I am unalterably rooted in native ground, they consider me a work of primitive art, housed in a magical color; the incarnation of civilization, anti-heathenism, and the fruit of a triumphing idea. They are coolly passionate and smile at me lecherously with speculative crystal eyes of bright historical blue. The French find me *charmant* and would like to paint a picture. The Italians, used as they are to the habit, concern themselves with the giant cockroaches in the latrines and give me hardly a glance, except in reproach for them.

I am, perhaps, as I should be. *Gloria Deum. Gloria in excelsis Deo.*

I am a wife of Christ, a wife of the Catholic church. The wife of a celibate martyr and saint. I was born in this township, a village "civilized" by American missionaries. All my life I have lived here within walking distance of the Ruwenzori mountains—mountains which show themselves only once a year under the blazing heat of spring.

2

When I was younger, in a bright blue school uniform and bare feet, I came every day to the mission school. "Good morning," I chanted to the people I met. But especially to the nuns and priests who taught at my school. I did not then know that they could not have children. They seemed so productive and full of intense, regal life. I wanted to be like them, and now I am. Shrouded in whiteness like the mountains I see from my window.

At twenty I earned the right to wear this dress, never to be without it, always to bathe myself in cold water even in winter, and to wear my mission-cropped hair well covered, my nails clean and neatly clipped. The boys I knew as a child are kind to me now and gentle, and I see them married and kiss their children, each one of them so much what our Lord wanted—did he not say, "Suffer little children to come unto me"?—but we have not yet been so lucky, and we never shall.

3

At night I sit in my room until seven, then I go, obediently, to bed. Through the window I can hear the drums, smell the roasting goat's meat, feel the rhythm of the festive chants. And I sing my own chants in response to theirs: *"Pater noster, qui es in caelis, sanctificetur nomen tuum, adveniat regnum tuum, fiat voluntas tua, sicut in caelo et in terra. . . ."* My chant is less old than theirs. They do not know this—they do not even care.

Do *I* care? Must I still ask myself whether it was my husband, who came down bodiless from the sky, son of a proud father and flesh once upon the earth, who first took me and claimed the innocence of my body? Or was it the drumbeats, messengers of the sacred dance of life and deathlessness on earth? Must I still long to be within the black circle around the red, glowing fire, to feel the breath of love hot against my cheeks, the smell of love strong about my waiting thighs! Must I still tremble at the thought of the passions stifled beneath this voluminous rustling snow!

How long must I sit by my window before I lure you down from the sky? Pale lover who never knew the dance and could not do it!

I bear your colors, I am in your livery, I belong to you. Will you not come down and take me! Or are you even less passionate than your father who took but could not show his face?

4

Silence, as the dance continues—now they will be breaking out the wine, cutting the goat's meat in sinewy strips. Teeth will clutch it, wring it. Cruel, greedy, greasy lips will curl over it in an ecstasy which has never ceased wherever there were goats and men. The wine will be hot from the fire; it will cut through the obscene clutter on those lips and turn them from their goat's meat to that other.

At midnight a young girl will come to the circle, hidden in black she will not speak to anyone. She has said good morning to them all, many mornings, and has decided to be like them. She will begin the dance—every eye following the blue flashes of her oiled, slippery body, every heart pounding to the flat clacks of her dusty feet. She will dance to her lover with arms stretched upward to the sky, but her eyes are leveled at her lover, one of the crowd. He will dance with her, the tempo will increase. All the crowd can see the weakening of her knees, can feel in their own loins the loosening of her rolling thighs. Her lover makes her wait until she is in a frenzy, tearing off her clothes and scratching at the narrow cloth he wears. The eyes of the crowd are forgotten. The final taking is unbearable as they rock through the oldest dance. The red flames roar and the purple bodies crumple and are still. And the dancing begins again and the whole night is a repetition of the dance of life and the urgent fire of creation. Dawn breaks finally to the acclaiming cries of babies.

5

"Our father, which art in heaven, hallowed be thy name, thy kingdom come, thy will be done on earth—" And in heaven, would the ecstasy be quite as fierce and sweet?

"Sweet? Sister," they will say. "Have we not yet made a convert of you? Will you yet be a cannibal and eat up the life that is Christ because it eases your palate?"

What must I answer my husband? To say the truth would mean oblivion, to be forgotten for another thousand years. Still, perhaps I shall answer this to him who took me:

"Dearly Beloved, let me tell you about the mountains and the spring. The mountains that we see around us are black, it is the snow that gives them their icy whiteness. In the spring, the hot black soil melts the crust of snow on the mountains, and the water as it runs down the sheets of fiery rock burns and cleanses the naked bodies that come to wash in it. It is when the snows melt that the people here plant their crops; the soil of the mountains is rich, and its produce plentiful and good.

"What have I or my mountains to do with a childless marriage, or with eyes that can see only the snow; or with you or friends of yours who do not believe that you are really dead—pious faithful who do not yet realize that barrenness is death?

"Or perhaps I might say, 'Leave me alone; I will do your work'; or, what is more likely, I will say nothing of my melancholia at your lack of faith in the spring. . . . For what is my faith in the spring and the eternal melting of snows (you will ask) but your belief in the Resurrection? Could I convince one so wise that my belief bears more fruit?"

How to teach a barren world to dance? It is a contradiction that divides the world.

My mouth must be silent, then, though my heart jumps to the booming of the drums, as to the last strong pulse of life in a dying world.

For the drums will soon, one day, be silent. I will help muffle them forever. To assure life for my people in this world I must be among the lying ones and teach them how to die. I will turn their dances into prayers to an empty sky, and their lovers into dead men, and their babies into unsung chants that choke their throats each spring.

6

In this way will the wife of a loveless, barren, hopeless Western marriage broadcast the joys of an enlightened religion to an imitative people.

The Flowers

It seemed to Myop as she skipped lightly from hen house to pigpen to smokehouse that the days had never been as beautiful as these. The air held a keenness that made her nose twitch. The harvesting of the corn and cotton, peanuts and squash, made each day a golden surprise that caused excited little tremors to run up her jaws.

Myop carried a short, knobby stick. She struck out at random at chickens she liked, and worked out the beat of a song on the fence around the pigpen. She felt light and good in the warm sun. She was ten, and nothing existed for her but her song, the stick clutched in her dark brown hand, and the tat-de-ta-ta-ta of accompaniment.

Turning her back on the rusty boards of her family's sharecropper cabin, Myop walked along the fence till it ran into the stream made by the spring. Around the spring, where the family got drinking water, silver ferns and wildflowers grew. Along the shallow banks pigs rooted. Myop watched the tiny white bubbles disrupt the thin black scale of soil and the water that silently rose and slid away down the stream.

She had explored the woods behind the house many times. Often, in late autumn, her mother took her to gather nuts among the fallen leaves. Today she made her own path, bouncing this way and that way, vaguely keeping an eye out for snakes. She found, in addition to various common but pretty ferns and leaves, an armful of strange blue flowers with velvety ridges and a sweetsuds bush full of the brown, fragrant buds.

By twelve o'clock, her arms laden with sprigs of her findings, she was a mile or more from home. She had often been as far before, but the strangeness of the land made it not as pleasant as her usual haunts. It seemed gloomy in the little cove in which she found herself. The air was damp, the silence close and deep.

Myop began to circle back to the house, back to the peacefulness of the morning. It was then she stepped smack into his eyes. Her heel became lodged in the broken ridge between brow and nose, and she reached down quickly, unafraid, to free herself. It was only when she saw his naked grin that she gave a little yelp of surprise.

He had been a tall man. From feet to neck covered a long space. His head lay beside him. When she pushed back the leaves and layers of earth and debris Myop saw that he'd had large white teeth, all of them cracked or broken, long fingers, and very big bones. All his clothes had rotted away except some threads of blue denim from his overalls. The buckles of the overalls had turned green.

Myop gazed around the spot with interest. Very near where she'd stepped into the head was a wild pink rose. As she picked it to add to her bundle she noticed a raised mound, a ring, around the rose's root. It was the rotted remains of a noose, a bit of shredding plowline, now blending benignly into the soil. Around an overhanging limb of a great spreading oak clung another piece. Frayed, rotted, bleached, and frazzled—barely there—but spinning restlessly in the breeze. Myop laid down her flowers.

And the summer was over.

We Drink the Wine
in France

(Harriet)

"Je bois, tu bois, il boit, nous buvons, vous buvez...."
They are oddly like a drawing by Daumier. He, immediately perceived as Old; she, Youth with brown checks. His thin form—over which the double-breasted pinstripe appears to crack at the base of his spine—is bending over her. His profile is strained, flattened by its sallowness; unrelieved by quick brown eyes that twitch at one corner and heavy black eyebrows lightly frosted with white. There is a gray line of perspiration above his mouth, like an artificial moustache. His long fingers are busy arranging, pointing to the words on the paper on her desk.

She is down low. Her neck strains backward, bringing her face up to his. She is a small, round-bosomed girl with tumbly hair pulled severely back except for bangs. Her eyes are like the lens of a camera. Now they click shut. Now they open and drink in the light. Something, a kind of light, comes from them and shines on the professor of French. He is suddenly amazed at the mixture of orange and brown that is her skin.

"En France, nous buvons *le vin!"* The force of his breath touches her. She draws in her own. It makes a gasping sound that shocks him. He springs upright. Something stiff, aghast, more like a Daumier than ever, about him. The girl is startled, wonders why he jumped back so fast. Thinks he does not want to mingle breaths with her. For a hot flurried moment she feels inferior.

The professor takes cover behind his desk. His eyes race over the other forms in the class. He wonders what they notice. They are even worse than adult foreigners; they are children. When they see him going to the post office underneath their windows they call their friends to come and look down on his balding head. In the classroom they watch him professionally, their brown eyes as wary as his own. The blue-eyed girl begs for, then rejects, kinship. With him. With them. Her skin is white as the ceiling. The brown and rose of the skins around her do not give her a chance to exhibit beauty. By the range of colors she is annihilated. For this he feels vaguely sorry for her. But it is a momentary pang. He is too aware of her misery ever to bring it up. Hearing the bell he turns from her. For a moment his eyes lock with those of the girl who never has her French. She is dreaming, has not heard the bell, is unaware. For a moment she drifts into his eyes, but the click comes and the eyes go blank. When she passes him at the door his heart flutters like old newspapers in a gutter disturbed by a falling gust of wind.

2

The professor goes by for his mail: it is a magazine and a letter from Mexico, where he will go as soon as summer comes. He can hardly wait to leave Mississippi for even greater sun. The surrounding beauty has crept up on him gradually since his arrival three years ago. He can no longer ignore it and it hurts him, terribly. In Mexico he will find an even slower-infecting beauty. When it becomes painful he will begin to explore countries even farther south. He has been chased across the world by the realization of beauty. He folds the letter, looks with horror at the narrow walls and low ceiling of the post office, rushes out into the bright sunshine.

3

Harriet is an ugly name. She wonders if it would sound better in French. She leans forward from the weight of six large and heavy books. She is not stupid, as the professor of French thinks. She is really rather bright. At least that is what her other teachers say. She will read every one of the thick books in her arms, and they are not books she is required to read. She is trying to feel the substance of what other people have learned. To digest it until it becomes like bread and sustains her. She is the hungriest girl in the school.

She sees the professor take out his mail; the letter, which he reads, and the magazine, which he sticks under his arm. While she scans the bulletin board noting dances to which she will not be asked the panic of his flight reaches her. She wonders if his letter was about someone who has died.

4

Later, in the car, her body is like a lump of something that only breathes. She feels her lover's hands, dry and young, rake up the impediments of her clothes. A thrust of one hand against her nipples, nearly right, then a squeeze that accomplishes nothing. She feels herself borne backward on the front seat of the car, the weight pressing her down, the movement anxious, selfish, pinning her, stabbing through. When it is over she is surprised she can sit up again, she had imagined herself impaled on the seat. Sitting up, looking out the window: "Yes, it was good"; she remembers not the movement knocking against her stomach but the completely correct account she has given the word *boire. Je bois, tu bois, il boit, nous buvons.* . . .

They move back toward the campus, she feeling outside the car, far away from the hands that manipulate the wheel. They hurry. If the gate is locked she will have to climb over the wall. For this she could be expelled. The boy sweats, worried about their safety, the future he wants. She thinks climbing walls an inconvenience but the humiliation of failure is not quite real. The knot behind her ear where a policeman struck her two weeks before begins to throb. But they are not late. She walks the two blocks to the campus gate, passes the winking guard, smells the liquor on his breath as he sniffs after her. She wonders about this injustice, her confinement, tries to construe an abstract sentence on the subject in impeccable French.

5

The professor will have cottage cheese, a soft egg, a glass of milk and cream for his meal. He has an ulcer and must take care of it. He wonders if Mademoiselle Harriet has noticed how he belches and strokes his stomach. He really must stop thinking of her. Must remember he is old. That death has had its hands on him. That his odor is of ashes while hers is of earth and sun. As he eats his colorless meal he remembers the magazine. It opens to his own story; a story he wrote to make the new pain less than the old. It is a story about life in a concentration camp. The same camp that gobbled up his wife and daughter and made fertilizer from their bones. He recalls the Polish winter, cold and damp and in his memory always dark; the stiff movement of the long marches, bleeding feet. It is all in the story; seven years of starvation, freezing, death. The publishers have described his escape in sensational language. His survival, in their words, appears abnormal. He is a monster for not now pushing up plants in the backwoods of Poland. A criminal for crossing Europe unslaughtered; for turning up in France already knowing the language. For having had parents devoted to learning that in the end had not done them any good!

The author is now Professor of French at a school for black girls in the Deep South.

Outraged, the professor flings the acknowledgement of his existence across the room.

6

"Mon Dieu, quelle femme!" Harriet inspects her naked body in the glass. She imagines that the professor will climb up the fire escape outside her window, that he will creep smiling through the curtains, that she will reach out to him all naked and warm and he will bury his cold nose and lips in the hot flesh of her bare shoulder. Undressed (she imagines him first in long red underwear), he will lean over her on the bed, looking. Then into bed with her. They will lie, talking. For there is no hurry about him. He is old enough to know better. He strokes her neck below the ear and tells her of his life. Explains the blue stenciled numbers she has seen peek from beneath his cuff—a cuff he is always adjusting. For she is ignorant of history. Her own as well as his. He must tell her why he put a tattoo there only to keep trying to hide it later. He must promise her he will not be embarrassed to remove his coat in class, especially on hot days when it is clear he is miserable. So much he must tell her. . . . But now her body has completely warmed him. His body seems to melt, to flow about hers. His mouth, fuller, plays with her breasts, teasing the nipples, light as the touch of a feather. His hands find, discover, places on her back, her sides. She takes him inside herself, not wanting to make him young again, for she is already where he at old age finds himself.

A knock, harsh and resounding, announces bed check and the house mother. Harriet has time to slip into her nightgown and mumble "Yes, ma'am" before the gray-brown dream-dispelling face pokes rigidly into the room.

7

Once in bed the professor abandons himself. He thinks hungrily of his stupid pupil. He remembers her from the very first week of classes; her blurred, soft speech, which he found difficult to understand, her slow comprehension—far behind the nearly white girl with the blue eyes, who ate French sentences choppily, like a horse chopping grass—her strange brown eyes so sorrowful at her ignorance they seemed capable of moaning. She is younger than the grandchild he might have had—and more stupid, he adds. But he cannot think of her as a child. As young, yes. But not the other way. She brings the odor of Southern jails into class with her, and hundreds of aching, marching feet, and the hurtful sound of the freedom songs he has heard from the church, the wailing of souls destined for bloody eternities at the end of each completely maddened street.

Her speech, which he had thought untutored and ugly, becomes her; the sorrowful eyes have bruised him where they touched. He dreams himself into her songs. Cashes the check from the story and buys two tickets to Mexico, lies with her openly on the beaches, praises the soft roundness of her nose, the deep brown he imagines on her toes, bakes his body to bring them closer to one. All the love from his miserable life he heaps on her lap.

When he awakes from his dream sweat is on his forehead, where years ago black hair curled and fell. And he is crying, without any tears but sweat, and when he turns his face to the wall he is already planning the wording of his resignation and buying brochures for South America.

8

"*Nous* buvons *le vin*," Harriet practices before entering the class, before seeing him. But the lesson for the day has moved on. It is "*Nous ne buvons* pas *le vin*" that the professor forces her to repeat before hiding himself for the last time behind his desk.

To Hell with Dying

"To hell with dying," my father would say. "These children want Mr. Sweet!"

Mr. Sweet was a diabetic and an alcoholic and a guitar player and lived down the road from us on a neglected cotton farm. My older brothers and sisters got the most benefit from Mr. Sweet for when they were growing up he had quite a few years ahead of him and so was capable of being called back from the brink of death any number of times—whenever the voice of my father reached him as he lay expiring. "To hell with dying, man," my father would say, pushing the wife away from the bedside (in tears although she knew the death was not necessarily the last one unless Mr. Sweet really wanted it to be). "These children want Mr. Sweet!" And they did want him, for at a signal from Father they would come crowding around the bed and throw themselves on the covers, and whoever was the smallest at the time would kiss him all over his wrinkled brown face and begin to tickle him so that he would laugh all down in his stomach, and his moustache, which was long and sort of straggly, would shake like Spanish moss and was also that color.

Mr. Sweet had been ambitious as a boy, wanted to be a doctor or lawyer or sailor, only to find that black men fare better if they are not. The South was a place where a black man could be killed for trying to improve his lot; the laws of segregation kept most black people from ever having decent schools, housing, or jobs. Since he could become none of these things he turned to fishing as his only earnest career and playing the guitar as his only claim to doing anything extraordinarily well. His son, the only one that he and his wife, Miss Mary, had, was shiftless as the day is long and spent money as if he were trying to see the bottom of the mint, which Mr. Sweet would tell him was the clean brown palm of his hand. Miss Mary loved her "baby," however, and worked hard to get him the "li'l necessaries" of life, which turned out mostly to be women.

Mr. Sweet was a tall, thinnish man with thick kinky hair going dead white. He was dark brown, his eyes were very squinty and sort of bluish, and he chewed Brown Mule tobacco. He was constantly on the verge of being blind drunk, for he brewed his own liquor and was not in the least a stingy sort of man, and was always very melancholy and sad, though frequently when he was "feelin' good" he'd dance around the yard with us, usually keeling over just as my mother came to see what the commotion was.

Toward all of us children he was very kind, and had the grace to be shy with us, which is unusual in grownups. He had great respect for my mother for she never held his drunkenness against him and would let us play with him even when he was about to fall in the fireplace from drink. Although Mr. Sweet would sometimes lose complete or nearly complete control of his head and neck so that he would loll in his chair, his mind remained strangely acute and his speech not too affected. His ability to be drunk and sober at the same time made him an ideal playmate, for he was as weak as we were and we could usually best him in wrestling, all the while keeping a fairly coherent conversation going.

We never felt anything of Mr. Sweet's age when we played with him. We loved his wrinkles and would draw some on our brows to be like him, and his white hair was my special treasure and he knew it and would never come to visit us just after he had had his hair cut off at the barbershop. Once he came to our house for something, probably to see my father about fertilizer for his crops because, although he never paid the slightest attention to his crops, he liked to know what things would be best to use on them if he ever did. Anyhow, he had not come with his hair since he had just had it shaved off at the barbershop. He wore a huge straw hat to keep off the sun and also to keep his head away from me. But as soon as I saw him I ran up and demanded that he take me up and kiss me with his funny beard which smelled so strongly of tobacco. Looking forward to burying my small fingers into his woolly hair I threw away his hat only to find he had done something to his hair, that it was no longer there! I let out a squall which made my mother think that Mr. Sweet had finally dropped me in the well or something and from that day I've been wary of men in hats. However, not long after, Mr. Sweet showed up with his hair grown out and just as white and kinky and impenetrable as it ever was.

Mr. Sweet used to call me his princess, and I believed it. He made me feel pretty at five and six, and simply outrageously devastating at the blazing age of eight and a half. When he came to our house with his guitar the whole family would stop whatever they were doing to sit around him and listen to him play. He liked to play "Sweet Georgia Brown," that was what he called me sometimes, and also he liked to play "Caldonia" and all sorts of sweet, sad, wonderful songs which he sometimes made up. It was from one of these songs that I learned that he had had to marry Miss Mary when he had in fact loved somebody else (now living in Chica-go, or De-stroy, Michigan). He was not sure that Joe Lee, her "baby," was also his baby. Sometimes he would cry and that was an indication that he was about to die again. And so we would all get prepared, for we were sure to be called upon.

I was seven the first time I remember actually participating in one of Mr. Sweet's "revivals"—my parents told me I had participated before, I had been the one chosen to kiss him and tickle him long before I knew the rite of Mr. Sweet's rehabilitation. He had come to our house, it was a few years after his wife's death, and was very sad, and also, typically, very drunk. He sat on the floor next to me and my older brother, the rest of the children were grown up and lived elsewhere, and began to play his guitar and cry. I held his woolly head in my arms and wished I could have been old enough to have been the woman he loved so much and that I had not been lost years and years ago.

When he was leaving, my mother said to us that we'd better sleep light that night for we'd probably have to go over to Mr. Sweet's before daylight. And we did. For soon after we had gone to bed one of the neighbors knocked on our door and called my father and said that Mr. Sweet was sinking fast and if he wanted to get in a word before the crossover he'd better shake a leg and get over to Mr. Sweet's house. All the neighbors knew to come to our house if something was wrong with Mr. Sweet, but they did not know how we always managed to make him well, or at least stop him from dying, when he was often so near death. As soon as we heard the cry we got up, my brother and I and my mother and father, and put on our clothes. We hurried out of the house and down the road for we were always afraid that we might someday be too late and Mr. Sweet would get tired of dallying.

When we got to the house, a very poor shack really, we found the front room full of neighbors and relatives and someone met us at the door and said that it was all very sad that old Mr. Sweet Little (for Little was his family name, although we mostly ignored it) was about to kick the bucket. My parents were advised not to take my brother and me into the "death room," seeing we we were so young and all, but we were so much more accustomed to the death room than he that we ignored him and dashed in without giving his warning a second thought. I was almost in tears, for these deaths upset me fearfully, and the thought of how much depended on me and my brother (who was such a ham most of the time) made me very nervous.

The doctor was bending over the bed and turned back to tell us for at least the tenth time in the history of my family that, alas, old Mr. Sweet Little was dying and that the children had best not see the face of implacable death (I didn't know what "implacable" was, but whatever it was, Mr. Sweet was not!). My father pushed him rather abruptly out of the way saying, as he always did and very loudly for he was saying it to Mr. Sweet, "To hell with dying, man, these children want Mr. Sweet"—which was my cue to throw myself upon the bed and kiss Mr. Sweet all around the whiskers and under the eyes and around the collar of his nightshirt where he smelled so strongly of all sorts of things, mostly liniment.

I was very good at bringing him around, for as soon as I saw that he was struggling to open his eyes I knew he was going to be all right, and so could finish my revival sure of success. As soon as his eyes were open he would begin to smile and that way I knew that I had surely won. Once, though, I got a tremendous scare, for he could not open his eyes and later I learned that he had had a stroke and that one side of his face was stiff and hard to get into motion. When he began to smile I could tickle him in earnest because I was sure that nothing would get in the way of his laughter, although once he began to cough so hard that he almost threw me off his stomach, but that was when I was very small, little more than a baby, and my bushy hair had gotten in his nose.

When we were sure he would listen to us we would ask him why he was in bed and when he was coming to see us again and could we play with his guitar, which more than likely would be leaning against the bed. His eyes would get all misty and he would sometimes cry out loud, but we never let it embarrass us, for he knew that we loved him and that we sometimes cried too for no reason. My parents would leave the room to just the three of us; Mr. Sweet, by that time, would be propped up in bed with a number of pillows behind his head and with me sitting and lying on his shoulder and along his chest. Even when he had trouble breathing he would not ask me to get down. Looking into my eyes he would shake his white head and run a scratchy old finger all around my hairline, which was rather low down, nearly to my eyebrows, and made some people say I looked like a baby monkey.

My brother was very generous in all this, he let me do all the revivaling—he had done it for years before I was born and so was glad to be able to pass it on to someone new. What he would do while I talked to Mr. Sweet was pretend to play the guitar, in fact pretend that he was a young version of Mr. Sweet, and it always made Mr. Sweet glad to think that someone wanted to be like him—of course, we did not know this then, we played the thing by ear, and whatever he seemed to like, we did. We were desperately afraid that he was just going to take off one day and leave us.

It did not occur to us that we were doing anything special; we had not learned that death was final when it did come. We thought nothing of triumphing over it so many times, and in fact became a trifle contemptuous of people who let themselves be carried away. It did not occur to us that if our own father had been dying we could not have stopped it, that Mr. Sweet was the only person over whom we had power.

When Mr. Sweet was in his eighties I was studying in the university many miles from home. I saw him whenever I went home, but he was never on the verge of dying that I could tell and I began to feel that my anxiety for his health and psychological well-being was unnecessary. By this time he not only had a moustache but a long flowing snow-white beard, which I loved and combed and braided for hours. He was very peaceful, fragile, gentle, and the only jarring note about him was his old steel guitar, which he still played in the old sad, sweet, down-home blues way.

On Mr. Sweet's ninetieth birthday I was finishing my doctorate in Massachusetts and had been making arrangements to go home for several weeks' rest. That morning I got a telegram telling me that Mr. Sweet was dying again and could I please drop everything and come home. Of course I could. My dissertation could wait and my teachers would understand when I explained to them when I got back. I ran to the phone, called the airport, and within four hours I was speeding along the dusty road to Mr. Sweet's.

The house was more dilapidated than when I was last there, barely a shack, but it was overgrown with yellow roses which my family had planted many years ago. The air was heavy and sweet and very peaceful. I felt strange walking through the gate and up the old rickety steps. But the strangeness left me as I caught sight of the long white beard I loved so well flowing down the thin body over the familiar quilt coverlet. Mr. Sweet!

His eyes were closed tight and his hands, crossed over his stomach, were thin and delicate, no longer scratchy. I remembered how always before I had run and jumped up on him just anywhere; now I knew he would not be able to support my weight. I looked around at my parents, and was surprised to see that my father and mother also looked old and frail. My father, his own hair very gray, leaned over the quietly sleeping old

man, who, incidentally, smelled still of wine and tobacco, and said, as he'd done so many times, "To hell
with dying, man! My daughter is home to see Mr.
Sweet!" My brother had not been able to come as he
was in the war in Asia. I bent down and gently stroked
the closed eyes and gradually they began to open. The
closed, wine-stained lips twitched a little, then parted
in a warm, slightly embarrassed smile. Mr. Sweet could
see me and he recognized me and his eyes looked very
spry and twinkly for a moment. I put my head down
on the pillow next to his and we just looked at each
other for a long time. Then he began to trace my
peculiar hairline with a thin, smooth finger. I closed
my eyes when his finger halted above my ear (he used
to rejoice at the dirt in my ears when I was little), his
hand stayed cupped around my cheek. When I opened
my eyes, sure that I had reached him in time, his were
closed.

Even at twenty-four how could I believe that I had
failed? that Mr. Sweet was really gone? He had never
gone before. But when I looked up at my parents I
saw that they were holding back tears. They had loved
him dearly. He was like a piece of rare and delicate
china which was always being saved from breaking
and which finally fell. I looked long at the old face,
the wrinkled forehead, the red lips, the hands that still
reached out to me. Soon I felt my father pushing something cool into my hands. It was Mr. Sweet's guitar. He
had asked them months before to give it to me; he had
known that even if I came next time he would not be
able to respond in the old way. He did not want me to
feel that my trip had been for nothing.

The old guitar! I plucked the strings, hummed "Sweet

Georgia Brown." The magic of Mr. Sweet lingered still in the cool steel box. Through the window I could catch the fragrant delicate scent of tender yellow roses. The man on the high old-fashioned bed with the quilt coverlet and the flowing white beard had been my first love.

New Paperback Editions from Harvest

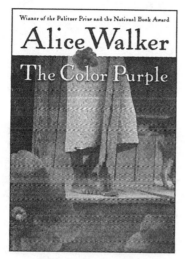

The Color Purple
$14.00 • 0-15-602835-2

Meridian
$13.00 • 0-15-602834-4

The Third Life of Grange Copeland
$14.00 • 0-15-602836-0

Her Blue Body Everything We Know
Earthling Poems 1965–1990 Complete
$15.00 • 0-15-602861-1

In Search of Our Mothers' Gardens
Womanist Prose
$15.00 • 0-15-602864-6

You Can't Keep a Good Woman Down
Short Stories
$13.00 • 0-15-602862-X